Praise for

DAWN of THE ICE AGE

"*Lug* is a stone-cold fun read. The talented David Zeltser spins
a clever prehistoric tale of friendship and adventure, with a
charming trio battling some fearsome bullies and beasts as the
Ice Age dawns. The humor is as sharp as the tigers' saber teeth."
**—Nathan Bransford, author of the Jacob Wonderbar
series and *How to Write a Novel***

"Any kid who's not extinct should love Lug's rough-and-tumble
romp through the world of dodo birds, jungle llamas,
and cavemen."
**—Anne Nesbet, author of *A Box of Gargoyles*
and *The Cabinet of Earths***

"David Zeltser's debut shows that courage takes many forms,
and that the struggle to fit in while being true to yourself
hasn't changed much in the past million years or so."
—Barry Wolverton, author of *Neversink*

"David Zeltser has unthawed a glacier of a story that will melt
your heart and leave you laughing out loud. Lug and his crazy
cast of supporting characters deserve five caveman clubs for this
hilarious saga of old traditions, dodo birds, and new beginnings."
**—Crystal Allen, author of *The Laura Line* and
*How Lamar's Bad Prank Won a Bubba-Sized Trophy***

"Suspenseful and smartly humorous, this novel delights with its
themes of brains over brawn and the power of friendship."
—*ForeWord Reviews*

BLAST FROM THE NORTH

by
DAVID ZELTSER

illustrations by
JAN GERARDI

❦ CAROLRHODA BOOKS
MINNEAPOLIS

Carolrhoda Books
A division of Lerner Publishing Group, Inc.
241 First Avenue North
Minneapolis, MN 55401 USA

For reading levels and more information, look up this title at
www.lernerbooks.com.

Main body text set in Garth Gothic Regular 12/20.
Typeface provided by Monotype Typography.

Library of Congress Cataloging-in-Publication Data

The Cataloging-in-Publication Data for *Lug: Blast from the North* is on file at
the Library of Congress.
ISBN 978-1-5124-0641-2 (TH)
ISBN 978-1-5124-0890-4 (EB pdf)

Manufactured in the United States of America
1-39324-21151-3/1/2016

For Aurora, Sage, and Naomi—
Never ever give up on making
your world a better place

And in loving memory
of Renato Dulbecco

—D.Z.

⊖ 1 ⊖

Heroes Don't Get Scared

"LUG!" yelled a screechy voice outside our family cave. "Lug, come see this!"

It was another freezing dawn—the time when old Crazy Crag usually had his big ideas. Last week it had been "moving pictures" on cave walls. The week before, something about an "ice eye" for seeing far away. As Crag ran around our snow-covered village's central clearing, shouting about his latest discovery, I yawned and snuggled deeper into my macrauchenia blanket. Whatever it was, it could wait until a more decent hour. Besides, I had just had another one of my bad nights. Ever since I'd helped rid our clan's territory of saber-toothed tigers last month, I'd been having terrible nightmares. Animals of every kind would chase me and try to eat me alive. Crag's shouts had woken me from a dream of being pursued by some very angry squirrels. Last night, it had been crazed dodo birds. I would usually wake up in a cold sweat, and my parents would ask what was wrong. But I was always too embarrassed to admit it. I wanted them to keep thinking of me as a hero, and I was pretty sure heroes weren't afraid of anything. Especially death by dodo.

"*Lug?*" repeated Crazy Crag as he entered our cave.

I closed my eyes and kept perfectly still. Crag would usually shout for a while before giving up and heading home.

"Asleep, huh?" he muttered. "Okay, what about your father? Big Lug, you up?"

I peeked out from under my blanket as he walked right up to my snoring dad, who was also the Big Man of our clan, the Macrauchenia Riders.

"Hey, Big Lug!" bellowed Crag, stomping the snow off his hide boots. "Come see this!"

"Whaaaaaat?" Dad yawned, rubbing his eyes and big bald head.

"Out there!" said Crag, pointing outside with an antelope horn. His bright blue eyes gleamed in the dawn light, and I watched his big bushy mustache twitch like a nervous squirrel's tail.

"Bonehead's gang come to steal another macrauchenia?" asked Dad, sitting up and starting to warm his hands over the fire pit.

Bonehead was a huge, nasty bully who—along with his sidekick, Bugeyes—had been known to swipe a jungle llama or two from the already dwindling herd in our clan's stable cave. Just before the final saber-toothed-tiger attack, Bonehead, Bugeyes, and their parents left our clan and became outlaws.

"It's not Bonehead!" screeched Crag. "Come up the mountain and see for yourself."

Dad glanced at my mother and sister, now looking up grumpily from their sleeping slabs. "Sorry, Crag," he murmured, placing a few thin slices of llama meat on a fire-pit stone, "I once forgot to make breakfast, and it was not pretty."

"Hey, Lug," piped up my sister, "maybe *you* should go." Windy was two years older than me and never missed an opportunity to boss me around.

"I can't," I muttered. "I have to work on a big cave painting for Echo's birthday."

"You know what I think?" said Windy. "I think you're *afraid* of going with Crag."

"No I'm not!"

My dad beamed at me, full of pride. "Don't be silly, Windy," he said, ruffling my hair. "Your brother here defeated a pride of saber-tooths."

"And Lug's very busy," my mother, Lugga, chimed in. "You have to remember that he's now our clan's Minister of Art and Culture."

"Whatever," muttered my sister, rolling her eyes. "He created that title for himself."

She was right. I had come up with that position last month after the Clan Council had asked me what I wanted. I figured that particular title would pretty much let me cave paint all day.

Crag narrowed his eyes at me. "Are you coming up the mountain or not?"

Suddenly, I felt something small and furry land on my shoulder. I jumped up and shrieked like a baby.

"Hey, hey! It's just Lumpkin," chuckled my dad. "What's the matter?"

"Nothing . . . nothing . . . " I said, trying to shake off our pet cave cat. "Just a little surprised."

But the embarrassing truth was that, ever since my nightmares had begun, I had secretly been avoiding animals. Even little Lumpkin freaked me out.

"Hey! Stony!" I called out in relief as my sleepy friend lumbered into the cave. "How's, uh, the new practice field coming along?"

Stony sat down by the fire pit and beamed a big bucktoothed smile at me. He had never spoken a word in his life, but an arch of his bushy unibrow could say a lot. It now twitched like a black cat's tail as he sniffed the sizzling meat. I glanced nervously at Froggy, the pet frog sitting on his shoulder, but said nothing.

After Stony had helped Echo and me defeat the saber-toothed tigers, he had also chosen a position for himself. Stony became the coach of our clan's headstone team, and had recently finished clearing a new practice field with two underground dugout caves to keep the players warm. Very useful when your previously grassy field is now permanently covered in snow.

"Here you go, Stony," said my dad, handing him a stick with a tiny slice of sizzling llama meat on it.

The changes in our climate had completely transformed our way of life. Our jungle llamas were dying out, and nobody had seen a dodo bird in months. Before, we had lived in a jungle of plenty, but now we were barely scraping by. With the onset of the permanent cold, it seemed like we were always just one step ahead of going the way of the dodo. When Bonehead and Bugeyes stole a jungle llama, it was a huge deal. Every little thing counted.

Stony scarfed down the morsel of charred meat and grinned.

My father smiled. "Hey, Crag," said my dad, "if you want to see a *useful* new discovery, you should try my new *cooked* meat. It's a big hit!"

Crag shook his head and exited the cave, shooting me one last exasperated look. Starving now, I decided I'd better grab a stick and dig in before my dad and Stony licked all the stones clean. I was just about to spear a sizzling morsel when I heard a familiar voice behind me.

"*Who* wants to try some *delicious* new vegetables?"

"Here we go again," said Windy, rolling her eyes.

We all turned back toward the cave entrance. Echo had come in, holding a bunch of weird-looking tuberous plants with pale, scraggly roots sticking out of them. Her curly red hair was dusted with snow and her big green eyes shone with what could only be called desperate enthusiasm. "Oh, come on now!" she pleaded, offering the plants. "None of you have even tried these!"

Everyone except me was trying to avoid eye contact with her. I exchanged a sidelong glance with Stony, knowing what was coming next.

"Look, I'm the Chief Enforcer for Ethical Eating," she said. "For *both* clans."

No one said a word. She was technically right, of course. The Joint Council of Macrauchenia

Riders (my clan) and Boar Riders (her clan) had allowed her to create a special position, just like me and Stony. Despite all my warnings that no one would take her seriously, she had made herself the Chief Enforcer for Ethical Eating. Basically, she went around and bugged people to eat vegetables instead of meat.

Echo had also created a "garden cave" with these strange leafy things. It was an abandoned stable cave where the dirt was full of old macrauchenia poo. Echo thought this somehow made her plants grow better. The cave also had many small holes in one sidewall, which let in the sunlight but kept out most of the snow.

"*Croak!*" went Froggy, leaping from Stony's shoulder onto Echo's.

The girl smiled fondly at the critter as he peeked at her from behind a curl of her red hair. I found myself staring at Echo's eyes, which got all twinkly when she was happy.

"*Croak, ribbit, ribbit, croak,*" said Froggy.

"*Ribbit, croak, croak, ribbit!*" replied Echo.

She loved animals more than anything in the

world and had a natural ability for communicating with them.

I cleared my throat. "Echo," I said, glancing at the hideous things in her hands, "would you like me to roast a 'vegetable' for you?"

Seeing that no one else was going to take one, she nodded and sat down by the fire with a resigned sigh.

I gingerly picked up one of the ugly things by a root and placed it on a hot rock at the very edge of the fire pit, as far away as possible from the actual food.

"By the way," said Echo, "I saw Crag storming out of here. What did he want?"

"Oh, you know, probably just wanted to show us some crazy new invention in his mountain cave. I'm sure it was nothing too importa—"

KABOOOOOOOOOOOOOOOOOOOOOOOOOM! The walls around us shook.

"Yeah," said Windy, "that didn't sound important at all."

We all crawled over to the mouth of the cave and peeked out. Stony grunted nervously as we gazed

up toward Mount Bigbigbig, which towered over our village. Despite the clear day, the mountaintop was now hidden in what looked like a giant snow cloud.

"What in stone's name happened?" asked Echo. Suddenly, a massive, shaggy, snow-covered beast lumbered out of the forest into our village clearing.

"Woolly!" cried Echo. She ran out and hugged the young mammoth's trunk. Ever since the mammoths had arrived with the cold, they had been helping our clans. Woolly had become a true friend. Now he looked from me to the mountaintop questioningly.

All eyes turned to me.

I swallowed the lump in my throat. "Well, I guess we'd better get up to the mountaintop and check it out!" I said, my voice cracking with false cheeriness.

To my chagrin, Stony, Echo, and Woolly all nodded in agreement.

≈ 2 ≈

THE CREEPING MOUNTAIN

BY THE TIME I walked over, Echo had already mounted Woolly and was whispering to him in the low, hushed rumblings of the mammoth language. Stony and Froggy were sitting just behind her.

"Thanks for coming to check on us, Woolly," I said, cautiously petting him on the trunk.

He nodded.

I glanced back at my parents. They smiled proudly.

Now I definitely had no choice. I clambered up

one of the mammoth's furry flanks and settled in just behind his massive shaggy head.

With Woolly's long loping strides, we quickly passed through the bare gourd-tree forest that surrounded our village and came to the main river— now frozen solid. The young mammoth carefully walked across it, and we were soon at the base of the mountain. It was nearly dark here in the strange snow cloud's shadow.

Woolly glanced back at us nervously.

"It'll be fine," I whispered, trying mainly to reassure myself. "Crag is expecting us up there."

The mammoth began to climb.

\\\\\\\\

The sun was high in the sky when we reached the windy, snow-covered mountaintop. Woolly stopped just short of the crest. As I climbed down his side, I thought I heard something behind me. Suddenly, I slipped in the snow, landing on my back.

"Are you okay?" asked Echo, offering me a hand.

"I'm fine!" I said, waving her away in embarrassment. I jumped up and slipped again, facedown this time.

She shook her head and walked off toward the nearby summit.

Stony tried to hide his smirk as he offered me his hand.

"*What?*" I muttered, spitting out snow.

"No way!" I heard Echo shout.

I quickly joined her at the crest and looked out over the northern valley ahead. Even the swirling snow could not hide the astounding sight that greeted us. Instead of the great white plain that we had all seen many times, there was now a brand-new mountain looming in the distance. Stony and I were too dumbfounded to even grunt.

"How?" muttered Echo. "How can a mountain just pop up?"

"*Creep,*" screeched a voice just behind us. "Not pop up. *Creep.*"

I wheeled around and slipped again. It was Crazy Crag, holding the long antelope horn to his eye and pointing it at the new mountain.

"Creep?" I said, brushing the snow off my hide coat. "How can a mountain creep?"

"Try my ice eye," he said, handing me the long horn. "Take a good look for yourself."

The horn had a beautifully curved piece of ice lodged in each end. Following Crag's example, I pointed one end of the horn at the distant mountain and peered through the other. "Whoa!" I said. "Everything looks amazingly close."

"Now point it at the bottom of the mountain. See how it's all shiny?"

"Yeah?"

"That's because it's mainly ice."

I moved the horn slightly downward and peered at where the ice mountain met the ground. "It's moving!" I said. "The mountain's just sliding over everything in front of it."

Echo grabbed the ice eye from me and peered through it. "It just crushed a tree like it was a twig!"

"Notice anything else?" asked Crag.

"Oh, stone it!" Echo whispered. "It's headed right toward our villages."

"*GLLAAAASHAAA*," rumbled Woolly, watching the creeping ice mountain.

"The mammoths call them glaciers," explained Crag. "They're common up north, but none of the mammoths in Woolly's herd have ever seen one moving this fast. My best guess is that it will crush both villages in four days."

I stared at him. "Um . . . Crag . . . when you say 'crush both villages,' do you mean—"

"Yes, Lug, *all* the caves. Every family's cave, your art cave, Echo's garden cave, even Stony's dugouts. *Crushed.*"

I looked over at Echo and saw her eyes start to well up.

"Wrong!" I blurted out. "We're not going to let it crush anything!"

Crag looked at me like I was a dodo bird that had just learned to talk. "Poor boy must have a fever," he said.

Stony put his hand on my forehead and grunted.

To be honest, I wasn't sure what had come over me either. "Well, we'll just have to go to this . . . *glacier*," I blathered on. "See what we can do about stopping it. I mean, what's the worst that can happe—"

KABOOOOOOOOOOOOOOOOOOOOOOOM!— an even louder explosion shook the ground and sent us all sprawling in the snow. Pieces of rock flew over our heads and pelted the slope of Mount Bigbigbig just below us.

"What was *that*?" I cried.

"*That*," said Crag, "is what happens when any pesky little thing gets in the glacier's way."

⊜ 3 ⊜

BLAST FROM THE NORTH

THE SUN SET as Woolly carried Echo, Stony, Froggy, and me down the northern slope of Mount Bigbigbig and onto the vast snow-covered plain below. A half-moon lit our way across the great expanse. With the tip of his trunk, Woolly also held a large burning torch that Crag had given us.

As we approached the glacier—now maybe twenty headstone fields away—Woolly suddenly halted, flaring his ears.

"What's the matter?" I asked.

Then I heard a faint sliding sound in the snow coming from behind a rise in the ground. We made our way to the top of the rise and looked down. I noticed the young mammoth staring intently ahead of him at an oddly shiny patch in the snow.

"What is it?" whispered Echo behind me. Stony was the first to clamber down, and Echo and I soon followed. We knelt by what turned out to be a sheet of thin ice about the same size as Stony. I gasped. I could see a boy's face just underneath the ice.

"Is he frozen?" Echo whispered.

He looked to be a year or two older than us and, in contrast to our light brown skin, his face was as white as a mammoth tusk. Unlike us, in our plain animal hides, he wore elaborate striped furs and a big spotted furry hat. He seemed to be holding a strange tuberous plant.

"That's one ugly vegetable," I muttered.

"Looks delicious to me," said Echo, getting up and grabbing the torch from Woolly's trunk.

"What are you doing?"

"Defrosting him."

"What . . . what for?"

Echo held the flame even closer to the ice.

"Wait!" I said. "What if he's dangerous?"

"What's he going to do, Lug, throw his vegetable at you?"

Stony giggled.

I sighed and watched the ice pool into water below her flame.

\\\\\\\

The first thing the boy did was throw his vegetable at me.

Moments before, I had decided to take a good close look at him. His eyes were shut underneath a few stray curls of light blond hair, but his thin lips seemed to tremble a little as if whispering some secret. I brought my face very near to his. Suddenly, he opened his eyes and threw his ugly vegetable at my head.

"Hey!" I said. "Watch it!"

"Hello there!" Echo greeted him, ignoring my protests. "I'm Echo."

The boy's thin lips curled into a delighted smile as he slowly stood up. "I am *Blast*," he said with a strange guttural accent and a graceful bow. "It is most pleasureful to meet you, Echo."

"I see you've already met Lug," she said. "And this is Stony, Froggy, and Woolly."

He gave them a bow and casually tapped his big spotted furry hat. I gasped again. The hat began to slowly unfurl, revealing itself to be a creature—like a mangy raccoon with a bad haircut and a rat tail. It gazed down at us with shiny black eyes.

"What is th-that?" I stammered.

"This is Doozy," said Blast. "My snow possum."

"Awwww," cooed Echo.

"Yah," said Blast, caressing the creature. "Doozy kept me alive in ice. You see, my people in North have expression: *No possum on head? You going to be dead.*"

"May I pet Doozy?" asked Echo, stepping forward.

The snow possum hissed at her, baring a mouthful of wet spiky teeth. Blast stroked the creature's head and whispered something into one of her pointy ears. With a resentful look, Doozy climbed into Echo's arms—her long ratlike tail wrapping around Echo's neck as if it were a tree branch.

I took a step backward. This thing was my worst nightmare come true.

🖋️

As Stony and I built a fire using the nearly burned-out torch, Echo stroked the snow possum and asked Blast where he'd come from.

"There!" he said, pointing at the creeping glacier in the distance.

Echo looked intrigued, and Stony made an

impressed whistling sound.

"Really?" I said, unable to keep the suspicion out of my voice.

"Yah," he said. "My people from North. I live on glacier with some good friends. But when dealing with some . . . pests, I fell and banged head on ice. Thereafter, you found me. Fortunately."

"Yeah," I muttered, eyeing Doozy, "fortunately."

Echo glared at me. She stood up and went over to where Blast's ugly vegetable still lay.

He smiled at her. "You would like to taste this last remainder of my edibles?"

"I'd love to!" she said, motioning for me to try it as well.

I shook my head and continued to stoke the little fire with Stony.

She took a nibble of the ugly thing and handed it back to Blast. "Mmmm," she said. "Delicious!"

"Yah!" said Blast, taking a big crunchy bite. "I am most pleased you like it."

"I only eat vegetables," she said.

"Me too!"

"I'm going to sleep," I muttered.

"Good night," they said in unison, without looking up at me.

I sighed. "Shouldn't we try to find shelter or something?"

"I not building anything tonight," snapped Blast.

I looked around at the few stunted trees in the snow. "Build something? What would we even build?"

Blast pointed at a large pile of snow against the side of a cliff. "Everyone in my clan know how to dig out cave from snowbank."

"How would that keep us warm?"

"You make small air hole, and the heat from bodies mostly stay inside."

"And you can do this?" I asked.

"Of course!" he snapped.

He sounded so defensive that I wondered if he really did know how.

"But fire will keep us warm enough tonight," he continued, turning away to add another stick to the flames.

꾸ㅣㅣㅣ

"Stay away from me, you freaky rat!" I screamed, sitting up in a cold sweat. "Oh, sorry . . ." I muttered as I realized that it was just Stony waking me from a nightmare. "I thought you were trying to bite my face off."

Stony flashed me his sweetest bucktoothed smile and helped me up. I looked around in the early dawn light and sighed in relief. Echo and Blast had their backs to me, stacking the last remains of unused firewood onto Woolly's back. The fearless way Echo had approached and handled the snow possum yesterday had made me feel extra wimpy. The last thing I wanted was for her to know about my silly animal nightmares. Then I noticed Echo running toward me.

"What's going on?" I asked.

"Blast found tracks around camp," she said.

"What kind of tracks?"

"Some terrible northern beast. Blast said we should head to the glacier for safety."

"And of course you believe him."

"Why shouldn't I?"

"Hmmm, let's see . . . how about because we

don't know anything about him?!"

"Lug," she whispered, "don't act like Bonehead."

I felt like I'd been slapped. Bonehead had been the biggest bully in our clan, until Echo, Stony, and I had defeated him last month. He was also about as smart as his name suggested.

"Take that back," I said.

"Um . . . many pardons," said Blast, walking up to us. "I hate to interrupt such nice chat but . . ." He pointed behind us.

I turned and saw what at first looked like a monstrous floating face in the distance. Narrowing my eyes, I saw the outline of a huge white beast, roughly the size of a saber-toothed tiger, but blending in almost perfectly with the snow around it. Whatever it was, it was bounding toward us, jaws open, huge teeth glinting in the morning light.

"POLAR BEAR!" Blast shouted.

⊖ 4 ⊖

A PACT IN THE SNOW

"ECHO!" I shouted. "Get on Woolly and ride back! We'll catch up to you."

"Are you crazy?" she replied. "I'm not leaving you guys."

I turned to tell Woolly to pick her up, but she started walking right toward the running bear— calmly, quietly, showing it her empty hands.

"Now who's *crazy*?!" I shouted. "What are you doing? That thing will kill you!"

Echo kept walking. "It's okay," she said to the

creature as it charged toward us. "It's okay."

"ECHO!" I screamed. "STOP!"

Amazingly, the bear shot right past her, like she was invisible. Then I saw its fierce dark eyes lock on to Blast. It bounded straight for him.

Blast reached into his fur skins and pulled out what looked like a big bone. I noticed that half its length was fire-hardened and looked very sharp— sharper than any piece of flint I'd ever seen. He took on a fighting stance, brandishing the bone knife.

The bear stopped just short of him, eyeing the blade warily. Blast tapped the snow possum with his empty hand. In a flash, Doozy leapt off his head and onto the bear's face.

The polar bear screamed with pain, shaking its head wildly as Doozy bit into its snout. Blast lunged forward with his blade, but the massive beast rolled out of the way just in time, sending Doozy sprawling in the snow.

The bear, bleeding from its snout, reared up angrily, towering over Blast. I took a step backward. Suddenly, a chunk of ice whizzed over my head and hit the bear right in the neck. The beast yelped and spun around.

A second ice chunk flew in from another direction and hit the bear just above its left eye. It staggered back toward Blast. Quick as a snake, Blast sliced his blade through the air, and connected with one of the pads on the underside of its paw. The beast roared in pain.

Bleeding, and clearly disoriented from the ice chunk to the head, the bear limped off as fast as it could.

"Now," said Blast, "we must get to glacier."

It dawned on me that Echo and Stony had thrown the ice chunks while I had stood there like a useless scaredy-cat.

"Wow, Blast," said Echo, catching up to him. "You're an amazing fighter."

"It is nothing," he replied, bowing slightly as Doozy climbed back onto his head.

"Who taught you to fight like that?" she pressed.

"Myself!" he blurted out. He seemed stunned for a moment, as if the answer had caused him pain.

"What about your clan?" I asked.

"*Not fighters*," he snapped.

"No? What are they, then?"

"They were . . . builders."

We all waited for him to continue, but instead he walked over and picked up the chunks of ice that had hit the bear. "Those were excellent throws," he said to Echo and Stony. "Do you practice?"

"Well, actually," replied Echo, "Lug had us throw hundreds of rocks at the saber-toothed tigers."

Blast arched an eyebrow at me. "You fought saber-tooths?"

"Um, yeah," I said, shrugging like it was no big deal. "I don't like to brag about it."

Blast eyed me thoughtfully for a moment.

"And Stony here is the coach of our headstone

team," said Echo. "That's a game that involves throwing stones—at other people's heads."

Blast looked at my silent unibrowed friend. "Really?" he said.

\\\\\\

After we'd put some serious distance between us and the polar bear, we finally stopped for breakfast. The glacier looked to be just a few headstone fields away now. Rather than risk attracting more unpleasant beasts with a fire, we sat on a tree stump and ate some of the dry food that Crag had given us. Stony and I shared some llama jerky, while Echo and Blast split the rest of his evil-looking vegetable. I cringed as Doozy's sharp teeth cracked through the bones of a snow hare she'd caught, devouring every last bit of it. She climbed back up onto Blast's head, kneaded his hair with her paws, and settled in for a snooze.

"Guys! I have idea!" announced Blast, suddenly standing up. "If you three crushed saber-toothed tigers, you can help me!"

"With what?" I asked.

"When glacier destroys your caves into tiny little pieces, your clans will need place to live, right?"

I turned to Echo. "You told him about that?"

She shrugged. "Last night, when you were sleeping," she said. "I thought maybe he could help us."

"And I *am* believing I can," he said. "If you help me scare off pesky polar bears, your clans can safely cross to glacier."

"Why would they *want* to cross?" I asked.

"To come have good life with my friends!"

"You mean *live* on the glacier?"

"It is not just *glacier*. It is full of the best, most spacious glacier caves. We will easily fit your clans."

"But the whole thing is moving!"

"That's right," he said with a little wink. "Never need to go anywhere. New adventures come to you. Echo—imagine you see new amazing animals every day. And Stony—imagine your headstone team can play new team every week. This beautiful dream can be your reality!"

They both started to look a little dreamy-eyed.

"What about food?" I asked.

"Food?" said Blast, smiling. "Well, you must come and see yourself!"

The idea sounded crazy to me, until I thought about how the glacier would destroy our villages. Where else were we going to move two entire clans in three days?

"Okay, Blast," I said, standing up from the tree stump. "We'll try to help you scare off the polar bears."

"Coooool," he said, flashing me a charming smile. "Very cool."

"But first let's see these glacier caves."

"Of course," said Blast, taking a step toward me.

I noticed that his snoozing snow possum was now peering at me with one half-open eye. I took a small step backward, hoping that Echo wouldn't notice.

"Lug," said Blast, reaching out, "we must clasp hands in honor of pact!"

With Echo now watching me, I had no choice but to step forward and shake his hand.

"Nice and warm," he said appreciatively.

I shivered at the iciness of his touch.

⊝ 5 ⊝

THE ICE CASTLE

WOOLLY REACHED the foot of the glacier and stopped at a stream of water running along its edge.

"What's that smoky scent?" I asked.

"Dinner!" said Blast, from the back of the mammoth. "You boys hungry for some meat, yah?"

Stony grunted with gusto behind me.

I looked up, past the stream, at the winding path that led up the glacier. It was surrounded by icy cliffs and barely wide enough for Woolly.

"But I don't see any fires up there," I said.

"And I have delicious vegetables for us, Echo," said Blast, ignoring my last remark.

I looked back at the knee-deep water that seemed to skirt the entire glacier. "I guess all this is coming from the glacier, then?"

"Of course!" Blast laughed. "Glacier is mountain of ice floating on its own meltwater."

"*Oh,*" I said, nodding. "So why does this glacier float so quickly?"

"How do you know it is 'so quickly'?" snapped Blast. "I thought this was first glacier you saw."

"The mammoths know," I said, patting Woolly. "They've never seen one move this fast."

"Who cares! What matters is making polar bears go bye-bye. Then we get *your* clans safely to glacier."

"But—"

"He's right, Lug," Echo interrupted. "We don't have time to worry about anything else right now."

"Fine," I said grudgingly. I gave Woolly a pat on the head, urging him to keep on moving.

The mammoth waded easily through the knee-deep meltwater and the glacier seemed to meet us halfway. We trudged up the winding path.

It was nearly sunset when we reached the top of the glacier and found ourselves peering down on a bowl-like valley in the middle of it. It looked to be about a dozen headstone fields across. In the center of the valley was a magnificent structure the size of a single field. It was carved entirely of ice.

"There!" said Blast. "The ice castle!"

I watched a thin tendril of smoke snake into the sky as we approached the glistening building. Then I saw the most amazing sight. On the gently sloped roof, larger-than-life ice sculptures of moose, woolly rhinos, and other strange northern creatures sparkled in the cold sunlight. At the very top, a giant sculpture of a snow possum stood towering above all—its pointy icicle teeth and long rat-like tail gleaming.

"Wow," I muttered, "whoever made those is a real artist."

"Maybe," said Blast disgustedly, "but they don't scare polar bears away."

He dismounted and touched Doozy. The snow possum unfurled, jumped down, and immediately tunneled into the snow in the direction of the castle.

"You will please pause here while I announce you to my friends, yah?" asked Blast. "It is northern hospitality."

I watched as the snow possum reached the massive ice door of the castle, well before her master. She began to scratch at it furiously. By the time Blast had walked up, four huge boys had opened it. They looked around warily as they greeted Blast, then closed the door as soon as he'd entered.

"Yah," I mimicked, "*hospitality.*"

"Lug," said Echo, "please don't ruin this."

I was about to ask what exactly she thought I was ruining when the door swung wide open, revealing Blast in the doorway. "Welcome, my friends!" he called out to us, with a grand sweep of his arm. "Welcome to home of your future!"

We dismounted Woolly and followed Blast into a great hall with towering carved ceilings. Along the dazzling bluish walls were brightly lit archways leading into dark tunnels. At the very end of the hall—which was about half the length of a headstone field—a fire blazed in a big stone-floored pit. I looked up and saw that the smoke was escaping through a hole in the high ceiling above it. Strangely, the fire was being tended by a small child. He had his back to us and was wearing some kind of furry black cape. I walked toward the fire.

As I passed the brightly lit tunnel entrances I noticed that their archways were not lit by wood fires. Rather, in each tunnel sat a large stone bowl full of some sort of thick whitish liquid. I glanced at each flame as I passed by and marveled at how little smoke these strange woodless torches produced.

As I approached the wood-fed fire in the pit, the small cloaked figure turned. He was no child. He was a bearded olive-skinned man with dark wavy hair, who happened to be the size of a six-year-old. He was mixing what looked to be herbs in a stone bowl.

"This is my friend Ugo," said Blast, coming up behind me. "He is excellent chef."

Ugo looked up at me with dark wary eyes, like a mouse searching the sky for a hawk. I nodded politely.

"Ugo," said Blast, "these are my new friends, Lug, Echo, and Stony."

Ugo cleared his throat. "It is nice to meet you all," he said in a melodic singsong accent that fully pronounced every sound. "Any friends of Blast's are friends of mine."

Odd, I thought, looking from Ugo's swarthy face to Blast's snow-white complexion. Their accents were just as different as their skin colors. I had expected Blast's friends to all be from the same clan. And there was the slightest hint of sarcasm in Ugo's tone, suggesting that maybe Blast didn't have as many friends as he let on.

"Where is the rest of your clan?" I asked Blast.

"My clan?" he said mournfully. "My clan was destroyed. I am only survivor."

"Me too," muttered Ugo. "My clan was destroyed too."

"Destroyed? By what?"

"By what you are standing on now," said Blast.

Ugo nodded solemnly. "Yes, this glacier crushed my village too."

"*Oh*," I muttered, suddenly feeling terribly sad for both of them.

"We're so sorry to hear that," Echo offered.

"Thank you," said Blast, looking at the floor.

There was a long silence.

"That's why," he added, "after we make polar bears go bye-bye, your clans must come onto glacier. We must save them."

I nodded.

"But no more sad talk," said Blast. "Let us dine!"

Ugo gave a slow, dignified nod and walked over to the closest wall. He picked up and shook a tangle of vines with thick icicles clinging to them. A sweet chiming sound rang out and echoed throughout the great hall.

Stony suddenly turned and stared intently at one of the tunnels.

"What was that?" asked Echo.

"What was *what*?" I replied.

Then I heard it too—a faraway high-pitched little squeal, almost like a baby. It was quickly drowned out by the sounds of music from the tunnels. Then voices, getting closer and closer. Soon the great hall had come alive with chatter, music, and dancing torchlight. I forgot all about the strange squeal as kids of every color and stripe emerged from the tunnels. They were dressed in stunningly varied ways, and many held the odd woodless torches. Most excitingly, they carried ice platters heaped with delicious-looking meats, fish, eggs, berries, and nuts, as well as various foods that I had never seen before. It reminded me of the plenty of our jungle before the cold. It was as if these people lived in a giant bubble, completely unaffected by what was going on outside. But how?

A tall dark-skinned girl with frizzy black hair and almond-shaped eyes tunelessly strummed a wooden stringed instrument as a chubby blond kid juggled snowballs to the rhythm. Oddly, there were no adults in sight, except for the child-sized Ugo. But these kids were the most colorful and merry-looking band of revelers that I had ever seen.

"Lug, Echo, and Stony, meet Boaga," said Blast. "She is our chief music maker."

I could tell that my friends were thinking the same thing as they smiled at the dark-skinned strumming girl. Maybe it would actually be fun to live here.

Boaga nodded at us, her topknot of frizzy black hair bobbing to the beat. A thick green vine swayed around her neck as she played her instrument. Suddenly, Froggy leapt off Stony's shoulder into Echo's hair, croaking in alarm.

The vine on Boaga's neck was still swaying to the rhythm even after she had stopped moving. I gasped and stumbled backward as the green snake uncoiled, peering at me with bright yellow eyes.

"Chill-chill, Lug!" said Boaga, chuckling. "Just my friend Scarf. He's already chow-chowed."

I took an exasperated breath and glanced around the room. Almost everyone looked amused, including Echo. Blast and Doozy were watching me with special interest.

"Okay, Blast," I said, "is *everyone* here wearing some freakish hidden creature?"

"No," said Blast, calmly stroking his snow possum. "Not *everyone*."

6

HIDDEN CREATURES

"ARE WE PLAYING a guessing game, Blast?" I muttered. "Who else has a hidden animal?" Echo elbowed me in the ribs as Blast just kept smiling.

"Just one more of us," he said. "But you've already met."

I glanced at Stony. He shrugged and shook his head.

"Ugo," said Blast, "stop cooking and show Lug."

The tiny caped man turned so that his back was toward me and lifted up his arms. His furry "cape" leapt off his back. I barely ducked in time as the big black shrieking bat whipped past my face.

Cringing, I watched as the bat swooped up toward the smoke hole in the ceiling—high above the fire—then dived back down toward its master. Ugo casually held out a hand, and the bat alighted on his forearm. Still, it kept its big black eyes on me.

"Oh, *Loo*-na," said Ugo, stroking the creature's veined leathery wings. "You are such a bad little bat."

Blast laughed heartily, but I was too freaked out to do anything but try to catch my breath. I felt like I was in one of my nightmares.

I glanced at Echo and Stony, now sure that they thought I was a coward. But they just watched, mesmerized, as Luna crawled up Ugo's arm to his neck and draped her wings over his back again.

And then—as if it was perfectly normal that there was a tiny chef with a huge bat on his back—the feast began.

\\\\\\\/

Stony went straight for the moose-meat platter and immediately ate most of it, grunting with pleasure. I saw Ugo carefully spicing and grilling some of the other meats with the herbs he'd prepared. I took a couple pieces of some kind of bacon from another platter. To my delight, I found it incredibly crisp and flavorful—even better than the best boar bacon.

"Can m'snake have the other piece?" a girl's voice said behind me.

I turned and found the tall Boaga looking down at me with her dark almond-shaped eyes. Her snake was even closer, eyeing my bacon with interest.

"It's his favorite," she explained.

"Sure," I said, handing her a slice and trying not to cower.

"Scarf and me appreciate that!" she said, looking surprised. "No one around here ever shares."

"What do you mean?"

She glanced toward Blast, but said nothing.

I watched Scarf scarf down the bacon in a single gulp. He then immediately began eyeing the half-eaten second slice I was still holding.

I had the strong urge to get as far away from this creature as possible, but then I heard Echo from across the fire pit. "Where do you get all these *amazing* vegetables?" she asked Blast.

"Come!" he said, taking her by the hand. "You must see to believe!"

I watched him lead her over to one of the tunnels, and they disappeared into it. I turned back and found Boaga watching me. "Let me guess," she said with a sly smile, "you want to see too?"

I nodded.

She looked meaningfully at the bacon in my

hand. "I may be able to tell you how to get there,"
she said.

I handed the slice to her, and Scarf immediately
snapped it up.

\ttttt/

After listening to Boaga's instructions, I had nearly
caught up to Blast and Echo. I followed their footsteps
through a dimly lit upward-sloping tunnel. I climbed
for a long time, winding around and around, until
it felt like I must be approaching the top of the
castle. Eventually, I came upon a thick ice door and
heard the unmistakable grunts of many moose. Not
much farther along was another ice door with what
sounded like woolly rhinos snorting behind it. As I
continued to follow Blast and Echo, I passed many
more stable chambers throughout the tunnel, each
with the sounds of different animals. Blast and his
friends were, by far, the richest group of kids I'd ever
met. But how had they gotten all these creatures?

At the end of the tunnel, Blast pushed open
another ice door. I shielded my light-dazzled eyes.
Blast and Echo entered a chamber, and I followed to

the doorway. A huge sunlit garden filled with lush green plants lay before me. I stared in awe at the light streaming through a ceiling of clear ice.

"Echo," said Blast, "welcome to my greenhouse!"

She walked around the huge chamber in wide-eyed amazement, gently running her fingers along every plant she passed.

"See those?" said Blast, pointing up at the ceiling.

I followed his gaze through the ice to some dark circular shapes on the roof.

"Are those rocks?" asked Echo.

"Ice chunks," said Blast. "I have told my friends to put those there for next time polar bears come to castle. You and your friends will aim from roof and hit bears on ground. Once bears are no longer problem, your clans can safely come to glacier."

Echo looked thoughtful. She bent down and smelled some little reddish flowers.

"In North we call those Little Reddish Flowers," said Blast. "They are same pretty color as your hair."

Echo smiled. "This place is wonderful. Did you help your clan build it?"

"Yah," said Blast quickly, then looked away. I

gulped as he peered in my direction, but he seemed too distracted to notice me. Then he spotted some small bright green-leafed plants next to him. He picked a few and handed them to Echo.

"What's this?" she asked.

"Mint."

"*Mmmmmmmm,*" she said, smelling it.

"Yah. Very good tea leaf."

"Tea?" asked Echo.

"Pull your possums!" he cried. "You never had tea?"

Echo shook her head, and her eyes got all twinkly with excitement.

He smiled.

When they began picking mint leaves together, I started to wonder if Echo was starting to like Blast more than me. He was obviously a big brave hero, and I was just a scared little kid. I turned around and slunk out without a word.

\|\|\|\|

I entered the great hall and saw that there were just a few children left, carrying the leftovers on ice platters back into the tunnels. Ugo was stoking the fire. I was relieved to see that his bat, Luna, looked to be sleeping, and decided to use this opportunity to ask some questions. As I approached, the little man turned and eyed me warily.

"So, Ugo," I said, "how do you like living on the glacier?"

"Fine," he muttered.

"That's good," I said. "And what do you think of the polar bears?"

"I don't think about them."

We both watched the flames for a while. The orange reflections dancing on the bluish ice walls were mesmerizing.

"Do you ever wonder what the polar bears want?" I asked.

Ugo continued to gaze at the fire. "Food, of course," he said.

"Just food, huh?"

He looked up sharply. "Why do you want to know?"

I noticed his bat stirring. "Well, you know, Blast has asked us to help get rid of the bears."

His lips tightened at the mention of Blast's name. "Hmmm," he muttered.

"Anything you can tell me will help us do the job."

Ugo's eyes narrowed. "The bears don't want to share the glacier with us," he said.

"But why? You don't seem to be competing with them for food. Seems like you have plenty of it stored away."

Ugo eyed me for a long time. "Where is your girlfriend?" he finally asked.

"She's not my girlfriend!" I snapped. "She's . . . my friend, who also happens to be a girl."

"Ah," said Ugo. "So where is your friend who also happens to be a girl?"

I swallowed a lump in my throat. "Right now, Echo is with Blast," I muttered.

"Good. So you know how it feels. The bears do not want any *other* land. They want the glacier. And we want the glacier."

He turned back to the fire, clearly done with me.

\\\\\

At night, strange smooth gray pelts were set on the floor, and many kids slept around the fire pit in the great hall. As I lay next to Stony and Froggy by the fire, my dreams kept bouncing back and forth between Echo and Blast in the greenhouse and Doozy chasing me.

I awoke to sunlight slanting through the huge ice door. Rolling over, I found Boaga smiling at me as she fried bacon on a hot rock in the fire pit. She picked up two slices and fed one to her snake. Then she handed the other one to me.

"Thanks," I said.

"No worries. You shared with us yesterday."

I noticed Echo was eating breakfast with Blast on the other side of the fire pit. After a while, a large boy ran up to him and whispered something in his ear.

Blast got up and looked around. "Polar bears are here!" he declared. "Lug and Stony, are you ready?"

"Stony's feeding Woolly," I said. "I can go get him."

"No time!" said Blast.

Echo and I followed him up to the greenhouse

and out through a hatch in its ceiling. Blast led us toward the already prepared pile of ice chunks at the top of the gently sloping roof. They were by the giant sculpture of the snow possum—its pointy icicle teeth and long rat-like tail gleaming in the morning light. Halfway down the roof was a slightly smaller but equally impressive sculpture of a woolly rhino. And looking down to the roof's edge, I could see the lifelike moose sculpture. These were so inspiring that I almost forgot about the real bears below. As a cave painter, I felt jealous of the artist's skill.

"Hey, Blast," I whispered as we reached the snow possum sculpture at the roof's peak, "who made these?"

"Shhhhh!" hissed Blast, suddenly annoyed. "If polar bears hear us, we are breakfast."

I looked down the other side of the roof and saw four polar bears sniffing around the castle's perimeter. They seemed to be oblivious to us. Blast picked up a few ice chunks from the pile, and Echo and I did the same.

"Aren't you worried they're going to smell us?" I whispered.

Blast looked from Echo to me, and sniffed the air. "Yeah, maybe they smell you," he said, and winked at Echo.

I took a deep breath—an icy roof was not a good place to lose your temper. I could see the smoke emerging from the hole to my left, and realized that we were directly above the great hall's fire pit.

"Awww," Echo whispered, "those bears are actually pretty cute from up here."

"Cute and deadly," said Blast.

"I'm sure you could take care of them on your own," I said, unable to resist, "with all your great fighting moves."

"Come on, guys," said Echo. "Everyone calm down."

"It is fine, Echo," said Blast. "Poor Lug—I know he is scared of my little Doozy. He must be SO scared of bears."

My jaw clenched and my eyes narrowed. That was the last thing I wanted Echo to know.

"So, Lug," he continued, "if you want to learn fighting moves, just ask."

"Fine!" I blurted out, grabbing for him.

He scooted back—quick as a rat.

I lost my balance. "Echo!" I shouted, reaching for her. But I missed her outstretched hand as I slid away. All the polar bears looked up at us.

"YOU IDIOT!" Blast screamed.

"You . . . you . . . *possumhead*," I said, as I slid toward the roof's edge.

7

ICE BREAKER

"I LOVE YOU, moose," I whispered to the ice sculpture. I'd grabbed onto its cold hoof at the last moment, and it was the only thing keeping me from falling as most of my body dangled over the roof's edge.

"Lug!" cried Echo. "Pull yourself back up."

"That occurred to me!" I called back. The problem was that I didn't want to pull too hard and crack the ice sculpture. That would have meant a plummet to certain death.

"Where's Blast?" I called up to her.

"Other side of the roof!"

I heard a scream and then a loud scrabbling sound. "What was that?" I asked.

"Oh no!" said Echo.

"Oh no, WHAT?"

"There's a polar bear on the roof!"

"WHAT?"

"I just told you what!"

"HOW?"

But before she could answer, Blast came scrambling over from the other side with an angry bear right behind him. I must admit it was actually enjoyable to watch.

"NOOOO!" screamed Blast as he slipped and started to slide.

Luckily for him, he slid by the snow-possum ice sculpture and managed to grab onto one of its feet, stopping his descent.

The bear roared in frustration as it slid past him, toward Echo.

She jumped out of the way, grabbing on to the horn of the woolly rhino sculpture for balance.

The bear roared even louder as it slid past her.

"No, no, no!" I muttered. It was coming directly toward me.

I pulled up on the moose sculpture's leg with all my might and managed to get my right foot back up on the rooftop. In a single frightened leap, I mounted the moose—just as the sliding polar bear crashed into its legs.

I cringed and waited for the legs to crack. When

they didn't, the polar bear regarded me with a puzzled look.

I flashed a nervous little smile. "How about we both count our blessings and call it a day?"

There was an ominous *CRACKING* sound at the top of the roof.

"PULL YOUR POSSUMS!" cried Blast.

I looked up to see the tail break off the snow possum sculpture.

"*Aiiiiiiii!*" screamed Blast as he slid down with it, crashing right into Echo.

The rhino sculpture's horn cracked off, and Echo and Blast continued down the roof together—directly toward me and the bear.

"Oh, COME on!" I muttered.

There was a jarring *CRASH*, followed by the *crack-crack-crack-crack* of the four moose legs. All of us went over the edge.

\\\\\//

"*OOOF!*" I grunted.

"Oww," murmured Blast and Echo in unison. I rolled over and saw that all of us had been lucky enough to land right on top of the now knocked-out bear.

"Uh-oh," I heard Echo mutter. I looked up and saw the three other angry-looking bears bounding toward us.

Then the ice castle's door swung open. It was Stony, his buckteeth gleaming in the morning sun.

Suddenly, the beasts halted and stared at the open door. Seeming to forget about us, they raced right past him into the castle.

"STOP THEM!" screamed Blast, charging after the creatures.

Echo and I ran over to the doorway and watched the bears sniff their way through the great hall. They seemed to find a particular archway they liked and disappeared into that tunnel.

8

DEEP DARK SECRETS

SOON THE POLAR bears reemerged from the tunnel. In each bear's mouth was what looked like a short-haired dog carcass, but with fin-like flippers instead of legs. The bears ran right past us into the snow. The knocked-out bear was just waking up, but soon caught up to the rest of the pack as they headed across the glacier. We watched as they slowly blended and disappeared back into the white landscape.

As Echo updated Stony on all that had happened, I walked around the backside of the ice castle. I saw a ramp that led up to the roof and realized how the bear had gotten up there. I walked back around to my friends and saw the shattered remains of the ice sculptures on the ground. Even the broken pieces were amazing to look at.

From behind me came the sound of quiet crying.

It was Boaga. She was kneeling down and running her fingers along the now-cracked woolly rhino horn.

"Boaga?" I said. "Are you okay?"

She nodded and tried to wipe away her tears.

"Wait," I said, "*you* made the sculptures?"

She nodded again. "I guess I'm better at art than music."

I picked up the beautifully carved rhino horn and examined it. "You're an amazing artist."

She smiled at me through her tears. Stony came over and started helping her pick up the pieces. Suddenly, Blast burst out the front door, followed by several large boys. He stared at the frozen landscape, fuming with rage.

"What were those things they dragged out?" I asked him.

"Seals!" he grunted.

"What are seals?"

"Stupid creatures that eat fish."

"So how do they survive in here?"

"We keep them frozen."

"Then—"

"No time!" he said, turning away in a huff. "You make big mess. Now I have to clean."

I watched him signal to the boys to follow. Then he stomped off down the length of the great hall.

"Good riddance," I muttered as he left.

"Are you forgetting that we *need* Blast to help our clans?"

I turned to find Echo behind me. "I think there's something suspicious about him," I replied.

"What?"

"I'm not sure," I admitted.

She rolled her eyes.

"What?" I demanded. "Are you best friends now?"

"Blast is trying to save our clans, Lug."

"I hope so."

She raised her eyebrows.

I sighed. "Okay," I said. "Fine. I'll try to focus on that."

"Good," she said. "Now, what do you think about sending Woolly back to tell Crag about everything that's happened so far? Crag can explain it all to our clans and lead them here."

"Yeah . . . I guess so."

"Great," she said. "I'll go talk to Woolly. Maybe you can try to patch things up with Blast? We've got to make sure he lets our clans onto the glacier."

I nodded, swallowed my pride, and went to look for him. I stopped short when I saw him talking to Ugo by the fire pit. I watched as the tiny man nodded toward one of the archways. Without another word, Blast hurried under it and disappeared into the dark tunnel.

I waited until Ugo had turned his back to the fire. Although Luna's eyes were closed, I watched the creepy bat for a moment to make sure she was asleep, then slipped into the tunnel after Blast.

Strangely, this one had no torches, and Blast had not carried one inside. The tunnel sloped downward and quickly turned pitch-black. I walked as fast as

I could, until I heard the sounds of Blast's footsteps echoing ahead of me. I tried to step lightly and could occasionally hear little animal-scampering sounds in some of the branching tunnels. I could feel the panic start to rise in my chest, slowly squeezing my breath out of me.

A high-pitched little squeal stopped me dead in my tracks. It was the same strange sound that my friends and I had heard yesterday, just before the feast. It was baby-like, except it had a pathetic yipping quality that I'd never heard a human make. There was something heartbreaking about it.

Blast's footsteps suddenly halted too. I approached slowly and peeked around a dimly lit corner. I saw a chamber illuminated by a single torch. Against one icy wall were piled dozens of the dead animals that Blast had called *seals*. I realized this must have been the place that the bears had targeted earlier, before they'd dragged the seals out of the ice castle.

"Lift it already!" hissed Blast. He stood in the middle of the chamber and addressed a huge muscular boy, who had his back to me.

The huge kid bent down and hefted what turned out to be a round cover made of ice, revealing a good-sized circular hatch in the ice floor. He set the heavy cover down like it was no big deal, and peered down into the hole.

Something caught my eye in the dim corner of the chamber. It looked like a cage with something small and white moving inside it.

"Where is your ugly helper?" Blast asked. "He supposed to be here always."

"Went for knife," grunted the huge kid, still keeping his back to me.

I know that voice, I thought.

"Plotting against me, eh?" said Blast.

The big kid shook his head, and hefted a big dead seal like it was a little cave cat.

"Throw it down, then!" commanded Blast, stepping out of the way.

"Okay," murmured the figure, maneuvering the carcass over to the hole and letting it go. It disappeared and, a few moments later, I heard a *THWAP* as it hit the floor somewhere below.

"Enough," said Blast. "Don't want to overfeed

them. And you gave them one yesterday for their torches, right?"

The huge kid nodded and turned sideways to pick up the hatch cover. My jaw dropped as I caught a glimpse of the foot-long bone through his nose.

"*Bonehead,*" I whispered to myself, pulling back into the shadows. It was the big nasty bully who had tormented our clan. He and his best friend, Bugeyes, had left last month and become outlaws. How in stone's name had Bonehead started working with Blast?

I peeked around again to make sure it was him. In the full light of the torch, I could see the bristle-skulled bully with his small watery blue eyes and the thin-lipped mouth that had more gaps than teeth.

Now I was sure that I had been right about Blast. Anyone working with Bonehead was clearly up to no good. I turned to run and tell Echo when a pair of horribly bulging eyes met mine.

"Bugeyes!" I cried. He was not as big (or dumb) as Bonehead, but he was twice as ugly, and with a surprisingly high-pitched voice.

"Hello, Little Slug," he squeaked, brandishing a large bone knife.

I backed away slowly.

Suddenly, I felt my legs kicked out from under me. I landed on my back with a groan. Scrambling up, I felt a big foot come down firmly on my chest. The "aroma" of Bonehead's feet was unmistakable.

"What . . . are you doing here?" I wheezed, trying to catch my breath.

Bonehead just smiled and grunted in satisfaction.

"Stupid Slug," squeaked Bugeyes, "who do you think told Blast about you and your little friends in the first place?"

"What?"

"Yah," said Blast, stepping into view. "Just before we first met, Bugeyes signal me that you are coming. And Bonehead cover me with ice shect."

"Why?"

"So you would think you *rescuing* me," Blast said. "That is why Echo and Stony trust me."

I looked over at Bonehead and Bugeyes. "We been watching you, Lug," said Bonehead. "Ever since you and your dumb dad took over *my* clan."

"It's not your cl—"

Bonehead leaned half his weight on my chest until I couldn't speak.

When he let up, I looked back at Blast. "What are you going to do to Echo and Stony?"

"Stony is idiot. Useless to me. But Echo, she will be *very* useful for getting your two clans here."

I flailed with all my strength, but Bonehead leaned the rest of his weight on me.

"Throw him in the dungeon," said Blast.

Bonehead and Bugeyes lifted me, turned me upside down, and dangled me over the open hatch.

"If you hurt my friends," I cried, "I will—"

"Drop him," said Blast.

My stomach lurched as I went into free fall.

⊜ 9 ⊜

DUNGEON OF ICE

"I'M ALIVE?" I whispered as I came to, lifting my head up and looking at the icy floor around me. "Hey, I'm *alive!*"

My nose wrinkled as I breathed in something stinky. I looked below me. "I love you, seal," I whispered to the soft carcass that had obviously saved my life.

I was in a huge ice chamber, illuminated only by the dim light coming through the hatch in the ceiling far above me. Yet, strangely, it felt much warmer down here. Nowhere near the chilliness of the great hall, and nearly as balmy as the greenhouse. There were several ice tunnels leading off the chamber. I picked the closest entrance and began to crawl toward it. Suddenly, I heard a loud *THWAP* behind me. I turned and saw a familiar figure splayed out on his back, on the same dead seal where I had just landed.

"Stony!" I said, rushing back. "Are you okay?"

He didn't move.

Then I saw that Stony's head rested against the dead seal's hard skull.

I shook his arm, but there was no response. "Come on!" I cried. "Please be okay!"

Stony lay dead still.

"Stony . . . *Stony* . . ." I began to sob uncontrollably.

"*Croaaaaak.*" A muffled sound came from underneath my friend's hand.

"Froggy!" I said, spotting the little guy and scooping him up.

"*Croaaaaak,*" repeated Froggy, plaintively eyeing his master.

Suddenly, Stony's chest rose ever so slightly.

"Stony?"

"*Croak, ribbit, croaaaaak!*" trilled Froggy. Stony was breathing.

"I'm going to try to find him some water," I called back, already heading toward a tunnel.

"That would be most delightful," said a deep voice.

I whipped around. Stony was sitting up and looking at me.

"Stony?"

"Indeed," he replied. "My deepest apologies for alarming you."

I stared at him. "But . . . but . . ." I stammered, "but you've never talked before!"

"I know," said Stony. "Puzzling, isn't it?"

"Um . . . *yes!*"

He wiggled his unibrow at me.

"Is it because you fell on your head?"

"Well, I believe a good tumble does sometimes knock a few stones loose," he said. "A highly improbable event, but there you have it!"

I nodded, even more amazed at *how* he spoke.

Stony looked around the huge chamber. "This place makes my dugout caves look like mouse holes."

"Stony . . . can you tell me what happened up there?"

He looked up at the now-closed hatch in the high ceiling. "I followed you," he said. "I wanted to make sure you were all right. Of course, I hadn't expected all this foolishness with Blast, Bonehead, and Bugeyes to transpire. When I confronted them—well, it appears manners are in short supply up there."

"Thanks for trying to help me," I said, offering him a hand.

Stony stood up and gave me a hug.

Then we headed out through the closest tunnel.

\\\\\\/

After some time exploring the dungeon's seemingly countless tunnels, we saw a faint light and heard what sounded like many flapping wings. We crept to where a tunnel curved, and craned our heads around for a peek.

I stared at the creepiest sight I'd ever seen. In the vast ice cavern ahead of us were dozens of people with bats clinging to their backs. All these folks—adults and kids—were very small, with olive-colored skin like Ugo, and most had the same dark brown wavy hair.

"Didn't Ugo say his clan had been destroyed by the glacier?" I whispered to Stony.

He nodded, still staring.

"Um, Stony, would you mind going in there and questioning these nice folks while I, uh, stand guard?"

Stony smiled. "Sure," he said. "And perhaps if we are successful in returning to the surface, I can help you overcome your fear of bats."

"I'm not afraid of bats!" I lied.

"It's okay, Lug," he said. "If one is not afraid, how can one overcome fear and become a true—"

"Stony!" I snapped.

"*Yes?*"

"I'm. Not. Afraid."

Even in the dim light, I could see the flash of his big bucktoothed smile.

꟫꟫꟫꟫꟭

It took me a long time to work up the nerve, but I finally walked into the cavern. To my horror, all the bats leapt off their masters' backs and flew toward me. I closed my eyes and shrieked like a baby.

After what seemed like the longest moment of my life, I tentatively opened one eye.

Big mistake.

I was instantly surrounded by fluttering, furry bits of darkness. I shrieked even louder as I felt the air from their flapping wings over my face and hands.

"Return!" boomed a man's voice, and the bats suddenly scattered.

I opened my other eye. All of the bats had returned to their masters.

The tallest man in the clan now stood before me. He was still shorter than Stony, but a little taller than me. His bat seemed to be whispering something into his ear.

"My Stella here believes you can be trusted," said the man. He spoke with the same singsong accent as Ugo, where every sound in the word was pronounced. "I am Renato, Big Man of the Batbacks Clan."

"I'm Lug," I said, trying to ignore his bat's piercing black eyes. "And this is my friend, Stony."

"So your clan was just captured, then?" asked Renato.

"Captured?"

"Yes. Have you figured out who betrayed your clan?"

I glanced at Stony. He arched a puzzled unibrow.

"May I ask," I said, "who . . . betrayed your clan?"

The man's face suddenly hardened like clay into stone. "We call him the *tiny traitor*," he said with disgust. "Perhaps you saw him up there?"

Stony and I looked at each other. "Ugo?" we both said simultaneously.

The man spit on the ground at the sound of the name. The rest of the clan did the same as the bats on their backs shrieked.

"Ah . . ." I said, backing away. "Well, thank you . . . We should probably get go—"

"Come!" said the little Big Man, motioning for us to follow. "Before you go anywhere, we must chew the fat."

I did not know what that meant, but it did not sound good.

⊜ 10 ⊜

THE BATBACKS

"MMMM," I SAID, taking the piece of seal blubber that Renato had handed to me, and trying desperately not to gag, ". . . chewy."

The little Big Man had led us back to the chamber where Stony and I had originally landed. We were sitting around the flame of a seal-blubber torch as two of his men cut the seal into pieces.

"Ugo is my brother," Renato explained. "But he is . . . different."

"Would you please elaborate?" said Stony, who

seemed to be chewing his piece of fat with great pleasure.

"Just like the noble bat, a true Batback must hunt prey and eat its raw meat to be part of our clan," explained Renato. "But several years ago, Ugo began violating our most sacred law by rubbing meat with plants, and placing it on fire! Of course, we banished him."

"For liking to cook?"

"It is not permitted," said Renato.

I glanced at Stony. This was starting to sound unpleasantly familiar—not unlike our banishment before the saber tooths had shown up.

"But instead of accepting his punishment honorably," continued Renato, "Ugo betrayed us."

"How?" I asked.

"When the glacier was coming down from the North and threatening our village, this nasty northern kid called Blast must have spotted Ugo on the outskirts. We think he got to know him and saw that Ugo might be willing to betray us. So, with Ugo's guidance, Blast approached us and promised that we could come and live on his glacier before it crushed us. Desperate for shelter, we agreed to have a look. Blast told us to bring all our sheep into the great hall. Then they took us down these dark winding tunnels, where Blast said we would be sleeping. Before we knew it, he had all our sheep, and we were trapped down here for good. That was about a year ago."

"But if his goal was just to take all your livestock, why would Blast continue to keep you alive?"

"That," said the little man, "is the great mystery." He gestured toward the dead seal his men were cutting up. "As you can see, Blast provides us with just enough food and fuel to survive."

"Are there other clans down here?" I asked.

"Oh, yes," said Renato. "From what I can tell, Blast found someone to betray each clan he encountered. Then he trapped the clans down here and, with the help of each group's traitor, stole all their livestock."

"I believe," said Stony, "Blast was hoping our clan's traitor would be you, Lug."

"*Me?* What about you?"

Stony arched his unibrow as if he'd just realized

something. "Echo," we whispered to each other in unison.

"We've *got* to get back up there," I said to Renato. "Our friend Echo has no clue that Blast is tricking her."

Renato shook his head sadly. "No one has ever found a way back up."

I peered at the covered hatch in the high ceiling.

"Don't even think about climbing," said Renato.

He was right—the walls were sheer, smooth ice.

\\\\\\//

Back in the Batbacks' campsite, we watched Renato prepare his hunk of seal so that a thick layer of blubber remained on the skin. He spread this out on the ice, with the blubber facing up to dry. As he handed his wife the remaining seal meat, Renato explained to us that once the blubber was dry, they would slice it up and render it for torch fuel.

"Fascinating," said Stony. "Have you considered cooperating with the other clans down here in order to find a way to escape?"

"Cooperating?" said Renato, shaking his head.

"No one down here trusts anyone else."

"Of course," I said. "You've all been betrayed."

Renato nodded thoughtfully and gave a furry morsel of seal skin to the bat on his back. "And, believe me, if anyone had gotten out of here, we'd all have heard about it."

"Where is the next closest clan?" asked Stony.

"Well," said Renato, hesitating, "I should warn you, they're pretty creepy."

I watched as his bat extended her wings and coughed up a big chunky hair ball.

"We'll take our chances," I said.

◒ 11 ◒

THE SNECKS

THAT AFTERNOON, Stony and I were peeking into an ice cavern full of dozens of people with snakes around their necks. In the middle of the floor was a huge pit full of writhing vipers.

"Stony?" I whispered hopefully.

"Sorry," he said, "my frog draws the line at serpents."

"But I didn't even ask anything yet," I protested.

"You know full well you were going to ask me to go down there and talk to those people by myself."

"Well, somebody has to stand guard."

"Yes," he replied, "the guy with the frog."

Against Renato's advice, we had sought out and found Boaga's clan by following the faint strains of music through many long dark tunnels. I swallowed hard and watched the tall people with frizzy black hair. Many were playing musical instruments as their snakes swayed to the rhythms. I took a deep breath and walked into their chamber.

Immediately, a large woman with a curled-up red snake around her neck and a stringed instrument in her hand came forward. "What's your song?" she asked, peering at me with her dark almond-shaped eyes.

"My song?"

"Each of us has a song," she said. "Do you know yours?"

I glanced back toward the tunnel where Stony was hidden, sure he could still hear our conversation. He stayed unhelpfully silent in the shadows.

"I'm sorry," I said, "but what is the name of this clan?"

"The Snecks," she said petting the snake around her neck.

"May I please speak with the Snecks' Big Man?"

"I lead the Snecks," she said, flashing a bright smile. "My name is Mammaga."

"Oh," I said. "So . . . you must know Boaga, then?"

Her snake lifted its head as the Big Woman's expression suddenly turned icy. "What about Boaga?" she boomed, bearing down on me. "How do you know the traitor?"

"Um . . . I met her . . . once," I said, backing into a wall. "Before Blast trapped me down here."

"What do you want?" she asked.

"Just a little help in getting us all out of here."

She seemed to relax a little, but she shook her head. "Luck be with you, boy," she said. "There's no way out for any of us."

"Maybe not alone. But what if you worked together with the Batbacks?"

"Why would we trust them? And, for the love of snakes, why would we trust *you*?"

I cleared my throat, trying to give myself time

to think. "Well we have a common enemy."

"Maybe," she murmured doubtfully.

"And . . . nothing else has worked."

She and her snake eyed me for a long moment. "Follow me," she said.

I glanced toward Stony in the shadows, but he didn't move a muscle.

\\\\\\/

As I sat surrounded by the rest of the Snecks Clan, Mammaga told me a tale very similar to Renato's. How Blast had convinced Boaga to betray her own tribe. How he had promised the Snecks that they could come and live on his glacier. How he had told them to bring all their goats into the great hall and had taken the people down through dark winding tunnels where he said they would be sleeping. And how he had disappeared and left them trapped.

Just like the Batbacks, the Snecks had no good answer for why Blast provided them with regular seal meat and kept them alive.

"But why would Boaga betray you in the first place?" I asked.

"I guess she never forgave us for banishing her," said Mammaga.

"I'm detecting a pattern here," I muttered under my breath.

Mammaga began strumming her instrument. Her snake swayed to the haunting melody. "You ever heard Boaga play?" she asked.

"Wait!" I said. "You banished her for not being *good enough* at music?"

"Music is everything to the Snecks," said Mammaga.

"But . . . she's really good at art."

"Tell me the truth, boy. You in league with Boaga?"

"No! I barely know her."

"Lug!" cried a familiar voice from one of the tunnels.

I turned wide-eyed, as did the rest of the tribe. "Boa . . . ga?" I stammered. "What are you doing here?"

She ran over and gave me a hug. "Blast found me making this ice sculpture of you," she said, handing it to me.

"Wow," I said, nervously examining the beautifully crafted sculpture, "I'm . . . pretty good-looking."

"Blast got very angry," she said. "He's always suspecting plots against him, and this made him sure of it."

"Boaga!" bellowed Mammaga. "How dare you come back here, *traitor*?!"

Boaga looked at her, her face full of righteous fury. "I'm not here for you. I'm here for my friend, Lug."

I looked from one to the other and managed a sickly smile. "Now everyone just calm—"

"Feed them to the pit!" Mammaga commanded. Suddenly, dozens of hands grabbed us. I struggled in terror as they dragged Boaga and me to the edge of the writhing pit of vipers.

"Toss them!" said Mammaga.

The crowd lifted us both over their heads.

"Wait!" I cried. "Don't kill your only hope!"

Mammaga raised a hand for the crowd to stop. "And who would that be?"

"Boaga here! She has gotten to know Blast better than anyone. She can help us."

Mammaga looked at me suspiciously. "You said earlier you barely knew her. Why would I trust you ever again?"

"Because, madam, I can vouch for him!" boomed a voice from the shadows. Stony emerged from a tunnel, beaming.

"Who in the Serpent of Truth's name are you?" asked Mammaga, now looking dizzy.

"I am a friend of the accused party," said Stony with great dignity. "And I know for a fact that Lug's intentions are pure and of the highest order."

Mammaga walked over and gazed down at the snake pit. "There is only one way to know for sure," she said.

"Uh . . . what's that?" I asked doubtfully.

"*Hissy!*" she said to the snake around her neck. "Bring me the Serpent of Truth!"

Mammaga's snake instantly uncoiled and slithered down her body to the floor, disappearing into the pit.

A few moments later, all the snakes in the pit began to hiss loudly. Then the writhing mass seemed to part into two halves as a snake the size of a banyan tree trunk slithered out toward Mammaga. The Serpent of Truth stopped directly in front of her, clearly awaiting further instruction.

"The little one!" Mammaga shouted over the deafening hiss, pointing at me.

I froze in horror as the huge snake wrapped itself around me, enveloping my body in its incredibly muscular coils.

☗ 12 ☗

SOUL SONG

"OKAY, LUG," said Mammaga. "What's your soul song?"

"My . . . soul song?" I croaked.

She strummed on her instrument. All the snakes instantly stopped hissing. Mammaga began to sing:

Every soul contains a sssong
And your song bessst be true
'Cause if it isn't, it isn't, it issssssn't
That snake is gonna eat youuu

The Serpent of Truth did not seem to like that
and squeezed tighter. This caused my mouth to open,
and to my surprise, I began to sing:

Suspicion's keeping us apaaart
But it's time to get over our fear
'Cause if we don't, we don't, we dooooon't
We're still going to be here next year

It felt like the Serpent of Truth was squeezing the song right out of me. The harder it squeezed, the louder I sang. Then its grip on me started to loosen, and I felt it swaying to my song. Amazingly, both Mammaga and Boaga began to sing along with me. By the time the snake had released me, the entire Snecks Clan had joined in.

"Sounds like we can trust you after all," said Mammaga.

\\\\\/

After much discussion that evening, the Snecks decided that Boaga would be pardoned for her betrayal, *if* she found a way to get them out of the glacier's dungeon.

That night, as I lay staring at the dancing flame inside a blubber-filled bowl, I tried to think. Boaga and Stony seemed to be having a snoring contest, which was not helping. Froggy was next to me, looking around warily. Night was the only time he could even think about coming out in Sneck territory.

I watched the Sneck people sleeping on their coiled snake "pillows." Suddenly, I noticed Boaga's snake, Scarf, uncoiling from beneath her head.

Boaga stayed asleep as Scarf darted off in the direction of a nearby tunnel. I didn't think much of it until I saw several other snakes doing the same. Soon, dozens of serpents were slithering away from their masters into the tunnels.

"Boaga," I whispered. "Boaga, wake up!"

She snored louder.

"Stony!" I said, shaking him. "Stony!"

He snored even louder.

"Great," I muttered to Froggy.

The frog, clearly freaked out by all the snakes, jumped onto Stony's face.

"WHO!" screamed Stony, leaping up into a fighting stance. This accidentally launched Froggy into the air. He landed on Boaga's face.

"WHA!" she screamed, jumping up.

"Take it easy, everyone!" I said. "You guys are like two dodos from the same nest."

Boaga narrowed her eyes as Stony flashed me a knowing smile. I picked up the trembling Froggy and tucked him into my sleeve.

"Where are all the snakes going?" I asked Boaga.

"Hunting," she said.

"Hunting what?"

"Just people."

Stony and I exchanged looks.

"Joking!" she chuckled. "People! Come on!"

I sighed in relief.

"Nowadays it's usually rats," she continued. "Before the cold set in, my Scarf loved a good frog when he could get one."

I felt Froggy move farther up my sleeve.

"Sometimes," she continued, "he'll snatch a slow bat."

"Really?" I said.

"Yeah, yeah! Scarf was always eyeing Ugo's bat. One time he almost got her. But Luna flew up-up-up to the ceiling."

"Up-up-up," I muttered to myself. "Up-up-up, huh?"

And then the idea hit me like a bat to the forehead. "Wait!" I cried, looking from Boaga to Stony. "That's it!"

Stony arched his unibrow questioningly.

"I've got it!" I said, jumping up. "I know how we

can get out of here!"

"Well?" asked Stony.

"I'll explain later," I said. "Right now, I need Boaga to teach me how to sculpt some ice."

"What do you want to make?" she asked.

"A weapon," I replied.

The next day, Stony, Boaga, and I stood before all the Batbacks and Snecks. It had taken some convincing to get the two clans into the same chamber, but we'd finally succeeded by explaining that we would need both bats and snakes for the escape.

"And, finally," I said, after outlining the entire plan, "we will need a volunteer! Which of you brave Batbacks is willing to be lifted and flown by a flock of bats through the hatch the next time Blast opens it?"

Laughter rippled through the crowd.

"What?" I muttered.

Renato raised a hand for silence. "Lug," he said, "if you want to try this craziness, you will have to do the flying."

"Oh no, no," I said. "There's no way."

"Why not?"

"Because I'm deathly afraid of your creepy little creatures touching me!"

Well, that's what I *wanted* to say. What I actually said was "I'm heavier than you."

Renato shrugged. "We have plenty of bats to spare for a little extra weight."

I eyed Boaga and Stony ruefully. Unfortunately, they were both heavier than me. I looked around the chamber at the hundreds of bats and imagined them clinging to me. "Maybe we should come up with another plan," I said.

"Of course," Renato said sarcastically, "let me know when you have one."

"Stony?" I asked hopefully. He shook his head.

I looked over at Mammaga and Boaga. They were still humming my soul song:

But it's time to get over our fear
'Cause if we don't, we don't, we dooooon't

"All right!" I cried. "I'll do it."

"Marvelous!" said Stony. "I'll spread the news to all the other trapped clans, so that they're ready for your return."

I nodded and turned to Renato. "Let's get your bats ready."

"Wait," he said, "there's one more thing. You'll need to smell dead."

"Dead?"

"Our bats like to pick up dead things and fly them out of the cave."

I stared at him.

"It's no problem!" he said. "We'll just roll you around in seal guts."

"How about you just kill me now?" I muttered.

⊜ 13 ⊜

WINGING IT

I PINCHED MY NOSE. I held my breath. I tried focusing my thoughts on getting out and rescuing Echo and our clans.

Nothing worked. It just really, really *stank* as two unfortunate Batback teenagers rolled me around in dead seal guts in the same spot where I'd originally fallen.

They ran off as quickly as they could. I stared up at the closed hatch in the high ice ceiling, listening intently for sounds up there.

A couple hours later, I heard faint footsteps above. I closed my eyes and gave a low whistle. From a connecting tunnel, I heard Renato shout: "Release!"

Soon I heard a flapping sound and felt something land on my leg. Then another bat flapped onto my chest. Two more bats descended on my head, tugging at my hair with their little claws. I felt the sweat trickling down my temples as more of the critters attached themselves to me. I had never been so creeped out in my life.

Eyes still closed, I heard the hatch slide open in the ceiling. This was the moment of truth. In another nearby tunnel, Boaga shouted: "Now, Scarf!"

I opened one eye and saw the big green snake race into the chamber toward me. The bats spotted it and shrieked in fright, flapping into the air.

"I'm flying!" I whispered to no one in particular. "I'm really flying!" Just as I'd hoped, the bats flew me toward the open hatch.

Suddenly, I saw a flash of red hair above me. It was Echo's head in the hole!

"If you are not helping me, you are hurting me," I heard Blast say. "I am sure you understand."

"All I understand is that you're a liar!" shouted Echo.

"Drop her," hissed Blast.

Now I could see him, Bonehead, and Bugeyes, each holding onto her body. The bats carried me through the hatch. I reached into my hide coat, pulling out my freshly sculpted ice sword. As I swung it around their heads, the bullies leaned back and let go of Echo.

"Lug!" she cried.

I grabbed her hand with my free one.

"YOU?" Blast shouted, but kept his distance from my sword. The stupefied look on his face was priceless.

Suddenly, there was a terrible squeal. Doozy had snatched a bat off my body and was eating it alive.

The rest of the bats screeched in fear and flapped even harder, flying me and Echo through the upper tunnel.

"Get them!" screamed Blast.

We had a good head start, and soon burst out into the bright light of the great hall.

As we passed the fire pit, a disbelieving Ugo cried, "HOW?"

"A bit batty, isn't it?" I shouted back.

"Luna!" hissed Ugo. His bat locked eyes with me and leapt off Ugo's shoulder after us.

I was expecting my bats to fly me and Echo up and through the smoke hole, but instead they flapped toward the castle door.

"Um . . . Lug?" cried Echo. "That door is closed."

"I noticed!" I said, taking a swing at Luna with my ice sword.

Ugo's bat swerved upward. To my horror, our bats circled back toward the tunnel we'd just come from.

"You plan even worse than you fight," said Blast, emerging from the tunnel. On his head, the snow possum was still chewing on a bloody wing.

Our bats shrieked at the sight, and suddenly rose toward the smoke hole in the high ceiling.

"Sometimes you've just got to wing it!" I shouted down triumphantly.

We burst through the hole and out into the frosty air, high over the ice castle.

"Luuuuuuuug!" cried Echo, her voice full of joy.

"Echooooooooo!" I shouted back.

It was a moment of pure exhilaration and freedom.

Then Luna shot out of the hole. Our bats responded by taking off across the glacier.

Luna zoomed toward us, clearly trying to scare our bats into dropping us. I thrust at her with my ice sword. She swooped up, and dived down at us again.

Thrust! *Swoop.* Thrust! *Swoop.* We repeated this aerial dance as we flew over the glacier.

I could now see our villages in the distance, and the edge of the glacier was ominously close to them.

Thrust . . . SNAP!—Luna clamped onto the ice sword's blade and bit it in half.

But the weight of it in her mouth caused her to plummet.

Exhaustion was slowing our bats too, and we were getting closer and closer to the ground.

Luna spit out the half sword and rocketed toward us again in a last-ditch effort to get the bats to drop us to our deaths. I threw my half sword at her, and she darted out of the way. Finally, our worn-out bats slowly descended to the ground, and deposited us safely in the snow. There was nothing Luna could do now.

﹌

A light snow began to fall as we watched Luna chase our exhausted bats back toward the ice castle.

"Wow!" said Echo. "Thank you, Lug."

"No problem," I said in my bravest-sounding voice.

Echo seemed to ignore this. "That all must have been really hard for you."

"What do you mean?"

"You know, because you're so afraid of bats."

I stared at her. "You could tell I was afraid?"

"I'm your friend, Lug. Of course I could tell. You've been afraid of most critters ever since we fought the saber-tooths."

My eyes went wide. "Wait," I said, "you knew I was a complete wimp this whole time? And you still wanted to be my friend?"

She shook her head. "Only crazy people don't feel fear. You're not a wimp. A wimp is someone who lets his fear stop him from doing what's right. A hero feels fear, but still does the right thing."

"*Oh* . . . I guess you're right."

"I usually am," she said, smiling.

"So . . . I'm a hero, huh?"

"Don't let it go to your head," she muttered.

"Too late!" I said, with a grin.

She wrinkled her nose. "What in the world is that smell?"

"Ewww!" I agreed, and then I realized that I was smelling myself. "Oh, that? You don't want to know." I picked up some snow and began to wipe down my face with it, hoping to get rid of the stink of seal guts.

"How long do you think we have before the glacier crushes our villages?" Echo asked.

"Maybe a day or so, at most."

"That's what I thought. And now our clans have nowhere to go."

"We'll think of something," I said as the snow came down faster and faster. "Maybe we should just make a mad dash for our villages now?"

She shook her head. "It's far too dangerous without a torch. We might have a better shot if we try to build a shelter first, and make a run for it when we can see better."

I looked at the bleak icy landscape. "But how are we going to build a shelter around here?"

⊜ 14 ⊜

CLAWDIA

WE WERE BOTH shivering when Echo pointed at a large pile of snow against the side of a cliff. "Lug," she said, "do you remember what Blast said when we first met him?"

"It is most pleasureful to meet you, Echo," I said in my best Blast imitation.

She grinned. "And then he said that if we dig out a snow cave with just a small air hole, the heat from our bodies will mostly stay inside and keep us warm."

"Yeah, but he never showed us how."

"No, Blast isn't much of a builder."

"Why do you say that?"

"When he took me to the greenhouse, he told me he'd built it," she replied. "But then I asked some questions about *how*, and he changed the subject. Anyway, I don't think digging out a snow cave is that hard."

"Let's do it!" I said, getting up and heading toward the cliff face.

"How's that look?" I asked as Echo climbed into the narrow tunnel I'd dug in the snowbank.

"Just a little farther," she said, pushing some more snow out.

"Hey, when did you realize for sure that Blast was a liar?" I asked, trying not to sound too happy about it.

"After you and Stony disappeared," she replied. "Blast said you guys had gone to summon your clan. I knew you wouldn't just leave me without saying something, so I searched for you all over the ice castle. Then, when Boaga disappeared, I told Blast I wouldn't bring my clan to the glacier unless he told me where the three of you really were. He gave me one of his charming smiles and told me to follow him. And that's when you found me—being thrown down the hatch."

I nodded and told her about how Blast had tricked and trapped the various clans at the bottom of the glacier. "But nobody understands why he keeps them alive," I explained.

Once we had dug the little snow cave, Echo crawled inside and began to smooth the inner walls. My job was to remove any extra snow that she pushed out of the entrance.

"It's ready," she finally said. "Come on in."

I took one more look around.

"Lug?" she called.

"Uh-huh?"

"I just wanted to say thanks again for rescuing me earlier."

"Don't thank me yet," I said.

"Why not?"

"Because there's a polar bear sniffing my face right now."

There was a long pause.

"Are you kidding?"

"I wish I was," I said as the polar bear sniffed my face.

"What's it doing now?"

"Dragging me away . . ." I squeaked as the polar bear hooked its teeth into the scruff of my hide coat.

I saw Echo's horrified face pop out of the snow tunnel. She began to run after us.

The bear picked up speed.

"Let him go!" Echo shouted, catching up.

The bear easily bounded ahead of her, and Echo began an all-out sprint.

"Drop him!" she cried. "Please! We're not your enemies!"

The beast just ran faster, and soon Echo was a small frantically waving figure in the distance.

I thought about trying to elbow the bear in the snout, but with its hot breath on my neck, upsetting it seemed like a very bad idea.

\\\\\

The polar bear carried me through heavy snowfall for I'm not sure how long. I was so exhausted that I may have drifted off and only opened my eyes again when the bear suddenly stopped.

"Hey!" I said, looking into a downward-leading tunnel in the snow. "What are you doing?"

The bear unceremoniously dropped me through the hole. I slid down the tunnel, and landed face-first in a sizable den. As I started brushing off my snow-encrusted face, I heard yipping sounds. They were just like the strange sounds I'd heard in the ice castle. Suddenly, I felt a raspy little tongue on my cheeks. I opened my eyes and saw a puff of white fur. A tiny bright-eyed cub was licking the snow off my face.

"Hello!" I said to the irresistible fluff ball. The cub yipped in delight and kept licking away.

I laughed. "Oh, you probably like my seal-guts smell, huh?"

I felt a jarring THUMP next to me. The mother bear had landed and she did not look as welcoming. I shot her an apologetic grin. She turned her backside toward me and sniffed her cub thoroughly, as if to make sure I hadn't hurt him. When she turned back, I noticed a bloody scab on her front paw.

"Oh!" I blurted out. "You're the one Blast cut."

She nudged the cub farther away from me. Then she turned and picked me up with her teeth again.

"Hey, wait!" I protested. "I've got to find Echo."

The mother bear carried me through a short tunnel, into a larger den chamber. Five adult polar bears and as many cubs watched me warily. Dim sunlight reflected in from various tunnels, but it felt colder in here than in the smaller chamber. The mother bear dropped me in the center. The largest male stepped toward me and growled furiously. His teeth were the size of my fingers.

The mother bear started pacing back and forth, making sounds at the others. She kept saying "*Whiska*" and imitating the baby-like yipping noises that I'd recently heard.

And that's when it dawned on me. "Blast!" I said. "Blast has taken one of your cubs, hasn't he?"

The bears all turned toward me.

"Oh, no, no," I stammered, "I wasn't involved." The female made the *Whiska* sound again, and then a deep rumbling in her chest.

I quickly began to trace a picture in the snow. I drew a figure with a snow possum on his head, holding a bear cub. The largest male stepped closer and glanced at the drawing suspiciously.

I pointed at the human figure I'd drawn. "Blast took your cub," I explained. Then I pointed at the figure of the cub. "Whiska?"

All the bears eyed me, but none looked particularly convinced of my innocence. The male made an ominous rumbling sound as he approached me. I thought it was all over when, suddenly, I felt an even louder rumbling from above. There was definitely something big on the surface.

The male bear pinned me against the den wall. He lifted his great white paw over my head, and I could see the enormous claws about to maul me.

"Wait!" said a voice from the smaller tunnel. "The boy's with me."

A tall thin snow-covered figure crawled in and dusted off his face, revealing a mustache like two frozen squirrel tails.

"Crag!" I cried.

The male bear looked from Crazy Crag to me, and back to him.

"Believe me, Clawd," Crag said to the bear. "He's on our side."

Clawd slowly lowered his paw.

Crag turned to the female bear. "Clawdia," he said, "I see you've all met my friend Lug, the world's most stubborn human."

"Hi," I said sheepishly, not sure if I should offer to shake someone's paw or what.

The mother bear continued to stare at me suspiciously. I shot a questioning glance at Crag.

"I found Clawdia bleeding from her paw a few days ago," he explained. "I nursed her wound and helped her back to her den."

Suddenly, the tiny bear cub ran in and started licking me again.

Crag smiled. "You've already met Puff, then?"

I nodded and started to thank Crag for coming.

"You can thank Woolly for finding me," he said.

I stared at him. "Woolly found you?" I asked, my heart suddenly sinking. "Then he delivered the message to you?"

"Yes," said Crag, "both clans are evacuating the village caves and bringing everyone to stay on the glacier."

"Stone it!" I muttered. "That was the message we'd given Woolly before we'd realized the truth about Blast."

"So Woolly delivered the wrong message?"

"I'll explain later," I said, heading for the exit. "First we've got to find Echo before she freezes."

⊖ 15 ⊖

A Flicker of Hope

WOOLLY WAS WAITING for us above the bear den. Crag and I mounted the young mammoth and rode back in the direction of the glacier. Fortunately, it had stopped snowing and it didn't take us too long to spot the figure of a shivering girl on the bleak landscape. Woolly wrapped his shaggy trunk around Echo and helped us place her on his back. We brought her back down into the warmth of the bear den. Once Echo was safe and sleeping, I must have collapsed in exhaustion.

When I opened my eyes again, the den was bathed in a faint glow of sunlight, and I found myself enveloped by the softest, warmest white fur. I stretched luxuriantly—as cozy as I'd ever felt in my life. Looking around, I saw that I was in the midst of a pile of snoring bear cubs, with the tiny Puff as my pillow. "I could get used to this," I murmured.

Across the den, Clawdia let out a desolate moan as she lay there. It was the miserable despairing sound of a mother missing her cub, and it brought tears to my eyes. I woke up Crag and Echo.

As Clawdia nursed Puff, the three of us hurriedly breakfasted on some of Crag's dried provisions.

"Turns out Blast imprisons any clan that comes to the glacier," I explained to Crag. "We didn't know that when we sent Woolly to you with the message."

Crag's eyes widened in realization. "So we have to go back and warn our clans to *stay away* from the glacier?"

I nodded.

"We better get going then," said Crag, standing up.

Echo went over to the miserable-looking mother

bear and gently stroked her back. "Clawdia?" she whispered.

The bear didn't look up.

"I really wish we could rescue Whiska," continued Echo.

"Maybe we still can," I said.

All eyes, including the bear's, were suddenly on me.

"What are you talking about?" asked Crag. "We have to go and warn our clans to stay away from the glacier."

"You don't need me to do that," I said. "I'm going back to the ice castle."

"Don't be a fool," said Crag. "You can't go there alone."

"I have to," I said, thinking of Stony, Boaga, and all the trapped clans.

"No, you don't," said Echo. "I'm going with you."

"*Neither* of you can go," said Crag, "because you won't have Woolly to take you. We need to ride him to get back to the villages in time."

Echo and I looked at each other. We had both forgotten that minor detail.

Suddenly, Clawdia stood up and walked over to me. The polar bear's big brown eyes gazed into mine, and I could see a flicker of hope there. She lowered her head, slowly, until her chin touched the snow. Then she gave me what was clearly a murmur of welcome.

I smiled and carefully climbed onto her back.

"This is madness," cried Crag. "I'm supposed to be the one doing crazy things around here! I'm Crazy Crag!"

"Crag—"

"How come I don't get to ride a polar bear?"

"Crag—"

"How come you guys go and do all this crazy—"

"Crag!"

"*What?*"

I pointed at the entrance to the chamber. Clawd had assumed the same position as Clawdia, welcoming Crag onto his back.

"You'll give me a lift to the villages?" Crag asked the big male bear.

Clawd nodded.

"Well . . . well . . ." muttered Crag, "that's good then."

Above the den, Echo clambered up onto Woolly. "We're back together, Woolly," she whispered, stroking his head.

"Thanks, crazy man, for all your help," I said to Crag, unsure when I would see him again.

He hugged me tight. "This is NOT good-bye," he said, wiping away a tear. Then he climbed onto Clawd's back. "Good luck!"

"Come on, Clawdia," I said, mounting up. "Let's go get your cub!"

Clawdia reared up and roared with enthusiasm. Clawd roared back encouragingly. Woolly stomped a foot and trumpeted.

As Crag raced back toward our villages, Echo and I rode off for the ice castle.

⊜ 16 ⊜

THINGS HEAT UP

"HOW DOES IT feel to ride a polar bear?" Echo shouted down from Woolly's back as we raced toward the glacier.

"Fun*aaaaaaaaaaah!*" I screamed as Clawdia bounded ahead of them.

The polar bear would periodically sprint far ahead of the mammoth. Then Woolly would catch up with his long steady strides, shooting me a slightly smug look as he passed us.

The sun was at its peak when we finally

approached the foot of the glacier. We dismounted and drank from the knee-deep stream of meltwater that ran along its edge. As I watched the glacier float toward us, I saw Echo pick up a small chunk of floating ice and stare at it.

"Lug!" she suddenly cried. "I think I know why this glacier moves so fast."

I walked over to her.

"See how my hand is melting this ice?"

"Yeah?" I said.

"Now, put your hand next to mine."

I did, and we watched the ice melt a little faster.

"It's people," she continued. "People are speeding it up."

"People?"

"You said that Blast trapped many clans down at the bottom of the glacier, and that it was warmer down there, right?"

I nodded.

"Well," she continued, "I think he traps people because people make heat. And Blast needs their heat to make the glacier melt and move faster."

I stared at her. "That would explain why Blast

feeds his prisoners and keeps them alive."

"And why he's so eager to get new clans trapped on the glacier," she said. "Remember how he had all those stable chambers?"

I nodded, remembering all the closed doors with the strange animal sounds coming out of them.

"My guess is that his own clan built the ice castle, and he stole it by trapping them."

"But why would he do that in the first place?" I asked.

"*That* I don't know," she said.

The glacier floated up to our feet. We both stepped onto its icy surface with a quiet *crunch*.

‖‖‖/

"I thought you said you had a plan," said Echo that afternoon, as we watched the sun light up a curling wisp of smoke above the distant ice castle.

"Not exactly," I admitted. "But the only way to stop the glacier is to stop it from melting, and that means we have to free all of Blast's prisoners. I think the only way to do that is to do what he least expects."

"And what would that be?"

"I'll walk right up and knock on his front door."

Echo cocked her head skeptically. "Just *you?*" she said. "What do I do? Braid Woolly's hair so he looks pretty for your getaway?"

"Well," I said, "do you have any better ideas?" It turned out she did.

\\\\\\/

When we reached the ice castle's door I asked Clawdia to lie down in front of it like she was a bearskin rug. Woolly used his trunk to cover Clawdia with fresh snow. Then the young mammoth carried Echo around back to the ramp that led up to the roof.

I took a deep breath and knocked.

After a while the front door opened slightly and three of Blast's cronies peeked out. They looked me up and down and saw that I was unarmed. Then one bounded off down the great hall as the other two shut the door on me.

It wasn't long before it opened again, swinging wide this time.

Blast stood in the entrance with his cronies

behind him. "Oh, *Lug*, did you forget something?" he asked, stroking the snow possum on his head.

"No, Blast," I said. "Just wanted to show you *my* hidden animal."

Blast smiled and pulled out his long sharp bone knife. "Ready," he hissed.

I tapped my foot, and the polar bear rose out of the white powder, lifting me high above Blast.

"B-bear!?" he stammered, stumbling backward and dropping his knife in surprise. He tried to recover it, but Clawdia was too quick, pinning him to the ground.

"Don't bother to get up—we'll let ourselves in," I said. "As soon as you answer a few questions."

Blast shot me a look of stone-cold hatred.

"First question," I said. "Where is the secret passage that leads to the bottom of the glacier?"

"What are you are talking about?" he hissed.

"The passage you used to trap all the clans," I said. "Where is it?"

"I don't know what—"

The bear growled directly into his ear.

"Remember Clawdia, Blast?" I said. "I know she remembers your knife. And we all know you stole her cub."

There was a long silence.

"There is small tunnel behind fire pit," he muttered. "That leads to bottom."

"And where is the cub?"

He hesitated for a moment. "Same place."

I caught Clawdia's eye and pointed to the end of the great hall, where Ugo was stoking a fire. The little man was watching us with wide eyes full of fear. On his shoulder, Luna extended her wings, ready to leap.

Clawdia lifted her great furry head, unpinning Blast, and carried me toward the fire. All of Blast's cronies backed up against the walls, making way.

"So, the conquering hero has returned?" hissed Ugo, eyeing the polar bear.

"Yes," I said. "And I was sorry to learn you were once unfairly banished by your own clan."

Ugo looked like I had struck him. But he quickly covered up his pain with rage. "If you weren't riding a bear," he snarled, "I'd throw you in this fire."

"Clawdia," I said, "why don't you show Ugo what we think of his fire."

The polar bear took a step forward, squatted, and peed on the flames, putting them out with a puff of steam.

Ugo's eyes narrowed into smoldering black holes. "How dare you?" he hissed.

"How dare *I*?" I said. "You have trapped your own people."

"If you have complaint about clan," came Blast's voice, much closer behind me than I expected, "you should talk to Big Man."

Clawdia and I whipped around.

"And I am Big Man of this glacier!" he hissed, slicing his bone blade dangerously through the air.

Emboldened by their boss's bravado, his cronies began to move toward us. They brandished icicles, bone knives, and ice swords. Even on a polar bear, I began to feel outnumbered and overpowered. Suddenly, there was a terrible shattering sound somewhere far above us. Everyone stopped and looked up.

"What was that?" Blast demanded.

"Nothing to worry about," I said. "Just a woolly mammoth shattering your greenhouse ceiling."

"Silly little liar!" he laughed.

I shook my head. "Echo's riding him. And you know how much she loves your vegetables."

"Ugo," said Blast, "take a few boys and check it out."

"Clawdia," I whispered, pointing to the tunnel behind the fire pit. "Now!"

With a single graceful motion, the bear leapt over the fire and bounded into the tunnel behind it.

"After them!" screamed Blast.

The dark tunnel curved sharply. Clawdia slipped on
the floor. I could hear her claws grating against the
ice as she barely caught her footing. She sprinted
faster and faster down the tunnel, and we spiraled
around and around. Finally, we reached what
seemed like a dead end. I could hear her desperately
sniffing the air for an exit, and the pursuing shouts
getting louder.

Clawdia gave a surprised grunt and pushed a
large block of ice out of a hidden opening between
two overlapping walls. This brought us into another
dark tunnel, which seemed even steeper and more
winding. It was much warmer here, just as when
I'd first fallen down the hatch. I smiled as I saw a
faint light.

Then a silhouetted figure with a possum on his
head emerged.

"Blast?" I cried. "No!"

17

THIN ICE

"DO NOT SPEAK the traitor's name," said the man's voice, in a guttural accent just like Blast's. "You must be Lug?"

I let out a sigh of relief, realizing it was one of the trapped members of Blast's own clan.

"Yes," I said.

"I am Gust. Big Man of Possumheads. The traitor's uncle."

"So then Stony got the message to all the clans?"

"Yah," said the man, "all are ready and waiting."

"Lug? Is that you?"

"Stony!" I cried out. "Follow my voice! We found the secret passage. Send everyone else through!"

\#\#\#\#

A few minutes later, Stony was climbing onto Clawdia's back behind me. "Nice ride!" he said. "Everyone is on their way."

"Wait for me!" cried Boaga, jumping onto the polar bear after him.

Clawdia turned and gave me a questioning look. She seemed unsure about Boaga's snake.

Suddenly, Blast burst in from the other side of the chamber, followed by several armed cronies.

"Boaga?" he said, shaking his head. "For a music maker, you are not very good listener."

Her snake hissed at Blast and his snow possum.

"Okay, Blast," I said, "where's Clawdia's cub? You said she was here."

"Did I? *Oops.*"

Clawdia stepped toward Blast and lifted a paw, roaring.

"No, Clawdia!" I shouted. "We need him to tell us where Whiska is."

The bear growled grudgingly.

Blast nodded. "Much better," he said. "Now close my secret passage, bear." He pointed to the large block of ice next to the hidden opening. Suddenly, we all heard the murmur of a crowd. It was the excited, disbelieving cries of trapped people about to be free.

"THEY COMING OUT?" Blast bellowed at me.

I smiled. *"Oops."*

"Let's go!" he screamed at his cronies, running back up the tunnel toward the surface.

Clawdia leapt after him as Stony, Boaga, and I clutched her fur for dear life. In moments, she was in front of Blast, blocking his path. He pulled Doozy off his head and threw the terrified snow possum at Clawdia's face.

As Doozy squeaked in fear and clung to the bucking bear's snout, Blast raced up the tunnel.

Clawdia roared and bucked even harder, sending Stony, Boaga, and me flying. We landed on our bottoms and skidded across the tunnel floor.

The possum and bear tumbled around in a shrieking whirlwind of white fur. I scrambled up and sprinted after Blast.

I burst out into the great hall just as Blast disappeared under another archway. Dashing after him, I soon heard shrill little baby-like shrieks echoing around me. I found this downward-sloping tunnel very familiar.

I followed the sounds of Blast's footsteps until I reached the chamber with the hatch in the floor. It was open and Blast held a squirming white baby bear by the scruff of her neck above the hole. "One more step," Blast hissed at me, "and baby go bye-bye."

I went for the cub, but strong hands grabbed me from behind. I lunged again. Blast straight-armed me in the forehead, sending me sprawling.

I fell backward—right into the arms of Bonehead and Bugeyes.

"Lug!" cried Echo as she entered the chamber. "Are you okay?"

I nodded, dazed but glad to see that Blast's cronies had not stopped her from entering the castle through the greenhouse.

I saw Blast's eyes dart sideways, and a scheming little smile came over his face. "Echo," he said, "it's not too late. We can still get out of here."

That snapped me right out of my daze. "Blast," I said. "It's over for you. All the people you've trapped are out by now. No one is heating the base of the glacier, and it's slowing down already."

"Not fast enough to save your villages," he said.

I looked at Echo.

"It's true," she said. "I was just up on the roof, and it doesn't look good."

Blast nodded at her, and offered his hand with a smile. "Join my crew, Echo. We can still get out of here together."

Echo looked at him. "I wouldn't leave Lug," she said. "But I will let *you* go if you hand over that cub and get out of here now."

Blast laughed. "Say bye-bye to Whiska, then."

Suddenly, there was a violent shaking and then—*KABOOOOOOOOOOOOOOOOOM!*—a great cracking sound from below. Bonehead and Bugeyes screamed and released me, and I heard the sound of rushing water beneath us. The glacier started to come to a *GROANING, CREAKING* halt.

"You slowed it too much!" screamed Blast, still holding on to the squirming cub.

"Just enough," said Echo.

Looking through the hole, I saw the giant chamber below filling up with water. I nodded. "Just enough," I said, "for it to sit on some boulder long enough to punch a hole through it."

"YOU RUINED MY GLACIER!" screamed Blast.

"*Your* glacier?" said Gust, entering the chamber.

Blast took a step backward. "Uncle?"

"What is the matter?" said Gust. "Weren't expecting to see your own people ever again?"

Blast's wild stare went from his uncle to me to Echo.

"Give us the cub," said Echo. "Whiska is innocent."

Blast shook with anger. "No!" he screamed, and threw the cub down the hatch.

Whiska squealed in terror as she fell and hit the turbulent water below.

"No!" cried Echo, and jumped in after the cub.

"Echo!" I called after her. The water was now

nearly up to the hole. Without thinking, I leapt in after both of them.

The freezing water made my breath come faster and faster. I began to sink and shiver uncontrollably. I looked around and saw a blurry Echo, halfway down, clutching a ball of white fur to her chest. I lunged toward them, swimming frantically.

But they were sinking to the bottom.

I felt my frigid body slowing down. I made another dive, even deeper, and missed them.

My vision started to go dark. I could feel myself starting to pass out.

No! I cried out silently and made one final effort, aiming toward them and kicking my legs as hard as I could. Suddenly, I felt Echo's hand in mine. A surge of energy and warmth shot through me. I pointed my head toward the surface and kicked my legs, pushing Echo and the cub in front of me.

I gasped as I surfaced. Blast was waiting for us. Bonehead and Bugeyes had pinned his uncle against a wall.

With a great strain, Blast lifted the icy hatch cover and prepared to seal us in a watery tomb forever.

I managed to push the cub up just in time. Whiska scrambled onto the ice . . . right into the paws of her *ROARING* mother.

Blast swung around in terror.

Stony stepped up, grabbed the hatch cover out of his hands, and THUMPED him over the head with it.

"That was the nicest sound I've heard Blast make," said Boaga, just behind Stony.

At the sight of the polar bear, Bonehead and Bugeyes took off running out of the chamber.

Clawdia quickly pulled Echo and me out of the water and brought us close to her chest.

"Thank you," I murmured, sighing in relief. When you're freezing, there's nothing like a bear hug from a polar bear.

⊜ 18 ⊜

A Doozy of a Day

ONCE WE'D WARMED UP, Echo and I went up to the roof of the ice castle to get a bird's-eye view of the situation. The glacier had stopped moving and butted up right against Mount Bigbigbig. Just below us there was a steady stream of newly freed men, women, and children emerging from the castle door.

"Who would have thought that *people* could melt glaciers?" said Echo.

"Yeah," I said, staring down at the happy crowd below. "And *stop* them from melting."

In the greenhouse we found Woolly waiting for us. I saw the mammoth-sized hole in the ceiling that he had bravely made to get Echo inside.

"That must have been fun," I said to her, examining the huge shards of ice that had come down when they'd crashed through.

"It was!" said Echo. "I'm just sorry we destroyed all these beautiful plants."

I looked around and noticed that the mint plants in the corner were untouched. That gave me an idea.

"Greetings, dearest Echo!" said Stony, entering the greenhouse behind us.

"Did you . . . just talk?" she asked, turning suddenly pale.

He arched his unibrow. "Indeed, I did."

She looked at me. "Am I dreaming?"

"Only," said Stony, "in the sense that each of our lives is but a fleeting dream."

"Better get used to it," I said to Echo. "He says stuff like that all the time now."

While Echo questioned Stony I quietly pulled out of some of the mint plants and tucked them into my hide coat.

The three of us led Woolly down into the great hall and met up with Renato, Mammaga, and the other tribal leaders. Gust and the Possumheads Clan had tied up Blast. He sat there on the floor, looking small and utterly defeated.

"Lug!" Gust called out. "As *you* are main force behind our clan's freedom and Blast's capture, you may decide how traitor will die."

"Has Blast admitted everything to you already?" I asked.

"Yah," said Gust. "He even told us why he stole cub from polar bears—a clan we have always respected."

"Why?" asked Echo.

"Blast was afraid to lose control over other traitors. So, he create common enemy for all of them to fear."

"Of course," said Stony. "He stole the cub so that the bears would constantly prowl around the ice castle, looking for her."

"Yah," said Gust. "This way, all other traitors had to focus on keeping the ice castle safe from bears. They had no time to think about how one *nasty banished traitor* controlled all of them."

"*Banished*?" I said. "Wait . . . Blast was banished *before* he did all this?"

"Of course," said Gust. "Two years ago he was banished from our clan for being a terrible builder."

I stared at Gust. "Go on."

"As people of the cold," he explained, "we prize above all else the ability to build great shelters. We teach children how to build small things very early, but Blast was always failure at this. So he was rightly banished to our glacier's dungeon."

"What happened then?"

"We threw down seal meat to keep him alive."

"How generous of you," I muttered.

"But Blast must have found a secret passage out," Gust continued, ignoring my sarcasm. "We all searched for him in dungeon. And that's when he closed up passage and trapped us down there."

I looked at Blast, but he did not return my gaze.

I glanced around at the Possumheads, and then at the Batbacks and Snecks. I saw Renato holding on to the captured Ugo—banished for not wanting to eat raw meat, and cooking. I saw Boaga—banished for wanting to make art instead of music.

I cleared my throat and spoke up. "Will every clan here allow me to pass sentence on these traitors?"

"Yes!" said Renato.

"Yes!" called out the leaders of the other clans.

"Then," I boomed, "I say *let them live!*"

There was a general commotion and cries of "Why?" and "But they betrayed us!"

I raised a hand for silence. The crowd quieted.

"You betrayed them first," I said. "Of course, that does not make their betrayal any more honorable. But it does make it more understandable."

The crowd began to murmur, full of discord.

"My friends and I were once banished!" I continued, gesturing towards Stony and Echo. "The three of us had each other, but not all kids are so lucky. When you banish people for their differences you cause terrible pain. And that pain can often come back to haunt you."

Mammaga stepped out of the now riled-up crowd. She was holding Boaga's hand.

A sudden hush descended.

"I am sorry, Boaga," she declared. "We were wrong to banish you."

146

"I am sorry, Mammaga," said Boaga. "I was terribly wrong to betray you."

A few in the crowd cheered as they embraced. Then Renato stepped forward. "Lug, on behalf of the Batbacks, I accept your judgment. Ugo shall live."

There was more cheering.

Now Gust stepped forward, and everyone's eyes went from him to Blast.

This time, Blast did look up. And there was the tiniest flicker of hope in his eyes.

Gust nodded toward me. "Blast shall live too," he said.

To my amazement, a collective sigh of relief came from the crowd, and a tearful Blast gave me a nod of gratitude.

\\\\/

Most of the clans were eager to have their livestock returned to them, and start the long trek back to their lands. But I invited the Batbacks and the Snecks to follow us to our village first.

Just before we left the ice castle, I remembered something. I asked Woolly to wait while I sprinted back inside. In the tunnel where Blast had thrown Doozy at Clawdia, I found the snow possum still lying there, staring at the wall in pain. I bent down and saw that her left hind leg was badly twisted out of shape.

I picked up Doozy. Her eyes widened with surprise, but she made no move to stop me. I took a deep breath and carefully tucked her into the warmth of my hide coat.

卌

I could smell the celebration starting long before we saw it.

"Lug!" cried my dad as we entered our village clearing. He and Stony's father were roasting an entire side of macrauchenia over a huge bonfire. Even Echo's dad, a less than friendly Boar Rider, had joined them. After reuniting with my family and reassuring them that I was okay, I took a break from the all-night feast and sneaked off.

The next morning, people were still drumming and singing, and many of the men were still eating. I caught sight of Mammaga, who thanked me and said her clan was ready to go home.

"Not everyone," I said, pointing with my torch. Mammaga and I watched as Boaga and Stony happily drummed on some rocks together.

"Down, Scarf, down!" chuckled Boaga, grabbing her snake. "You may not eat Froggy." Stony winked at me.

"Hmmm," said Mammaga with a sly smile, "maybe we can arrange for Boaga to stay a little longer."

I walked over to Echo and wasn't too surprised to find her playing with Puff and Whiska. It looked like she was trying to teach the poor things to eat vegetables.

"With all the commotion," I said, "you might think everyone's forgotten it's your birthday today."

She looked up in surprise.

"I have a present for you over there," I said, pointing toward her garden cave.

I felt nervous as she followed me. "Hope you like it," I said, and lifted my torch to the mouth of the cave.

She stared wide-eyed at all the mint plants I had saved from the destroyed greenhouse, now happily growing near the entrance. I entered and shone the torch on the walls, which I had just finished painting sky blue, with white clouds, black birds, and a yellow rising sun.

"I love it!" she cried.

"You do?"

She nodded. "And you know what I'd like to do more than anything in my garden cave?"

"What?"

"I'd like to share a vegetable with you!" she said. "Right now."

To my horror, she pulled a hideous pale thing right out of the ground—its little scraggly roots sticking out—and handed it to me.

"Um . . . uh . . . okay . . ." I stammered.

"I'm kidding, you fool," she said, hugging me.

I opened my mouth, but no words came out as I hugged her back. I was just happy. Very happy. Stone-cold crazy happy.

Then we heard a *squeak*.

"What was that?" she asked.

I looked down knowingly at my hide coat.

"No," she whispered in disbelief.

I opened my coat, and Doozy peeked out. "In my clan," I said, mimicking Blast's accent, "you must have possum to be awesome."

Echo laughed. "But, wait, Lug, aren't you afraid she'll bite you?"

We both looked at Doozy. The snow possum flashed a tiny toothy smile.

"A little," I admitted. "But that's what makes it kind of fun."

⊜ ACKNOWLEDGMENTS ⊜

Big thanks to the following possums for being awesome:

Alix Reid, Carol Hinz, and the Lerner team for saving the day! Catherine Drayton, Andrea Cascardi, and Jordan Hamessley for their early vision and editing prowess. Jan Gerardi and JP Coovert for the art. My writers group—Anne Ylvisaker, Carol Diggory Shields, Elin Kelsey, Jill Wolfson, Kate Aver Avraham, and Paul Fleischman—for the support and potlucks.

Special thanks to Benjamin Arthur, Brenda Leach, Carla Brown, James Aschbacher and Lisa Jensen, Judith Morgan, Julia Chiapella, Perry Hernandez and Ann Speno, Peter Lerangis, Ron Goodman and Song Nelson, my sister Sarah, my wonderful wife Fiona, and our parents, Maureen, Tamara and Alex.

To my readers and supporters—my gratitude.

To my friends and family—all my love.

⊖About the Author⊖

David Zeltser is the author of *Lug: Dawn of the Ice Age* and the acclaimed picture book *Ninja Baby*. An animal lover, he has worked with dozens of species of birds, rounded up stray giraffes with a pickup truck, and helped care for a baby rhino named Emmitt. David lives with his family and many barking sea lions in Santa Cruz, California. Follow him on Twitter @davidzeltser and www.davidzeltser.com.

〳〡〡〡〢